RESCUE DOGS

DUSTY

RESCUE DOGS

DUSTY

JANE B. MASON
AND SARAH HINES STEPHENS

Scholastic Inc.

Copyright © 2020 by Jane B. Mason and Sarah Hines Stephens

ISBN 978-1-338-36206-0

10 9 8 7 6 5 4 3 2   20 21 22 23 24

Printed in the U.S.A. 40
First printing 2020

Book design by Stephanie Yang

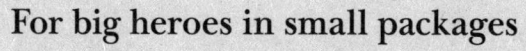

For big heroes in small packages

01

A black-and-white puppy snuffled along the edge of a dark road. The little dog was no bigger than a soda can and had to brace himself to keep from being tumbled in the wind whenever a car zoomed by on the two-lane highway. The headlights from each passing vehicle briefly lit up the dog's large, upright ears before quickly disappearing down the road into darkness. The pup barely looked up when he heard them approaching . . . he just locked his short legs and kept his black-and-white speckled nose close to the ground, sniffing through trash, leaves, and dry grasses. He was looking for food.

Looking for food—and water and shelter—was the

little dog's full-time job, and his only chance for survival. It had been a dry, hot summer, so everything was covered with a layer of dust. He nosed a gritty scrap of paper to get a second, closer sniff. The paper might have had food on it at one time, but the smell had faded. There was nothing to eat there, so he kept walking. The night was moonless and the pup had only his nose to rely on. Luckily smell was the keenest of his sharp senses—his nose rarely let him down. He drew in a breath and paused. This time he was certain he smelled *something*. It wasn't much, but something was always better than nothing. He and his pack had gone with nothing for too long.

The little dog paused to listen for his mother and two sisters. They were just a short distance down the roadway, also looking for food. His stomach rumbled. He froze and lifted a paw. It hurt. All of his paws hurt. His ears twitched, unable to hear his pack rustling through the roadside debris.

Back the way he'd come, there'd been a stronger food smell, a smell so strong it made his mouth water and the hunger gnawing his insides almost impossible to bear. But the smell had come from the middle of the pavement, and the middle of the pavement was a dangerous place. It was a place for zooming cars and big trucks and buses that smelled like gasoline and metal and oil. It was no place for a dog. He'd ignored the gnawing in his stomach and moved on.

The dog's ears twitched again, straining to hear his mama and sisters. They were coming along behind him more slowly than usual. He put his nose to the dirt on the edge of the road. Maybe he could find enough food for all of them.

The pack had been together since the three puppies were born. It was all the family the black-and-white pup knew, and he always felt safer when his mother and sisters were close by. Even when they were too hot or too cold or too tired or too hungry, they could curl up together and sleep. The sounds of his littermates breathing and his mama's heartbeat made him feel secure. It reminded him of the first days when they lived under the porch of the little casita behind the big house on the edge of the city, where the mama dog had crawled in to give birth and stayed to raise her puppies. It was nice there . . . cool and dark. The puppies had milk to drink, and there was a young girl who found them and brought his mama food, filled an old bowl with water, and held the puppy and his sisters. She kept the pup's little family a secret for as long as she could.

When the girl's parents found out what their daughter was up to, they put a stop to it. There was already a dog in the big house, a dog that barked at anyone who approached. They didn't want a stray and her puppies. They chased the pack away and put fencing around the porch so they couldn't get back in.

After they were evicted, the mama and her pups had taken shelter wherever they could: under trees, inside culverts, beneath boxes. Nobody brought them food or water. Nobody held them. Nobody took care of them. There were other dogs living on the streets, too. Lots of them. Some were friendly and some were not. All of them had to look out for themselves.

The little pup paused on the roadside. He lapped

up a few drops of water condensed on the underside of an aluminum can. The puddles had dried up between the brief spells of rain. The drops were not enough to quench his thirst. Still, they moistened his tongue.

Headlights appeared again in the distance, and a few minutes later a noisy car raced past. The pup braced himself but was blown back. He tumbled away from the road. Standing to shake himself off, he smelled something new—carne! The smell was strong and this time he did not hesitate to alert his pack. *Food! Here! Come get it!* he barked.

The sound was swallowed by the rumble of a bus barreling closer, then drowned out entirely by the squeal of brakes. A horn blared and the smell of burned rubber filled the dog's tiny muzzle. A dark and frightening feeling filled his chest.

The pup crept back through the dark toward the spot where the bus had stopped on the pavement. The giant machine heaved, like it was letting out its last breath, though its headlights still shone in the darkness. It shuddered and went silent. The doors opened and the driver descended. The pup drew closer. He couldn't see anything much beyond the hulking bus through the trash and dry weeds on the roadside.

Suddenly a woman's voice broke the silence. She was barking angrily. The pup craned his neck and saw the head and shoulders of a young woman with a young man beside her. They'd gotten out of the bus to talk to the driver, who stood silhouetted in the headlights with one hand on his head.

"Get back on the bus," the driver shouted at the woman in Spanish. "There's nothing you can do here. These mongrels shouldn't be in the road. They're nothing but trash!" he growled.

Even in the dark the puppy could tell that the girl didn't like the man's words. Or what she saw. She stared in the direction of the lights and held her stomach with one arm. She held her other hand over her mouth. After a moment she took it away to howl a reply to the driver. Her voice sounded wounded. Hurt.

All three of the people kept their eyes on the road

in front of the bus. They seemed frozen. They could not look away.

The pup snuck closer but stayed in the ditch, in the trash. He knew how to keep out of sight to avoid the kicks and brooms of the people who didn't want him nearby. He raised his head as high as he could to try and see what the people were looking at. He rose up for a moment, balancing on his back legs, and instantly wished he hadn't. With his nose high he smelled blood. With his eyes above the trash he saw his mama and sisters lying on the pavement. They were not moving. The woman let out a sharp wail, and the puppy swallowed his own. His pack was gone.

He was all alone.

02

Sylvia wiped an angry tear from her pale face. She turned her head from the awful sight and stepped to the edge of the road, wondering how the bus driver could be so heartless. He had struck and killed a mama dog and her puppies. All three animals were dead and he just seemed . . . irritated!

Sylvia's boyfriend, Xander, followed her to the side of the road. He didn't know what to say to make it better. Sylvia seemed sad and mad at once, and also as if she might explode. He reached a hand out toward her long black hair and then stopped, running it through his own short thick hair instead.

Swallowing more tears, Sylvia attempted to gather herself. She told herself it was an accident. The road was dark. There were no streetlights. The driver simply hadn't seen the small dogs. It wasn't as if he'd been *trying* to hurt them. And it was true that there were a lot more strays in Mexico than she usually saw in California. She'd noticed that when she'd come south to visit her family before. She'd also noticed the groups and shelters working to educate people and neuter the strays—to make the dog population stable and safe. But none of that kept the bus driver's words from echoing in her head. He'd called the black-and-white Chihuahuas "trash," as if discarding them to live on the streets was okay. As if they'd chosen to be hungry and alone. Only desperation would make a dog search for food on a highway. Sylvia felt her face go hot. She clenched her teeth together to keep from screaming.

She'd given the driver a piece of her mind in perfect Spanish, which seemed to surprise him. With her relatively light skin, it was not always obvious her parents were Mexican, and she liked being able to catch people off-guard when they mistook her for a basic gringa. His raised eyebrows and half-open mouth didn't bring any satisfaction today, though. The situation was too upsetting.

And now he was telling her to get back on the bus in Spanish instead of English. Most of the passengers were still on board, their faces pressed against the glass, watching.

Xander put his hand on Sylvia's arm and tried to tug her gently back on board. "I'm sorry to say it, but he's right, Sylvia. There's nothing we can do now. We're almost to your aunt and uncle's town . . . we should just get back on the bus."

Sylvia dropped her head and took a shaky breath. She wished she were back in San Luis Obispo, at school. Maybe it was a mistake to try to squeeze in a visit before the semester started. She wished she didn't get carsick. She wished she hadn't had to sit at the front of the bus. She wished she had never seen . . . any of this.

Staring at the ground in the dim light cast by the

bus, Sylvia saw something move. A piece of litter near her feet trembled in the windless night. She leaned closer. The tip of an ear stuck out from under the paper. "What the . . ." Sylvia bent down and a second ear joined the first, this one missing a small triangle of flesh, the fur-covered skin scarred over. A head two sizes too small for the ears emerged beneath them and a pair of dark, round eyes blinked up at Sylvia.

"Look at you!" Sylvia whispered. She squatted down quickly and reached out a hand. The black-and-white puppy cowered, stepping back and trembling slightly. But he did not run. "You must be . . . were you with—" She covered her mouth before she could say it. The puppy on the dusty roadside looked just like the two lying next to their mother on the road . . . not moving. "Oh. No," she gasped.

The small dog locked eyes with the young woman. He tried not to shake. Her eyes glistened. They were as wet as a puddle. When she reached out a hand he stayed as still as he could. She reminded him of the girl from the casita, the one who used to hold him.

He trusted young people more than old, probably because of that girl. But deep down he didn't trust people at all. He had suffered at the hands of humans more often than he'd felt comfort . . . a lot more often. Still, he stayed where he was.

"¡Vámonos!" the driver yelled impatiently from the steps of the bus.

"Are you all right? We have to—" Xander reached out again to try to coax Sylvia up and onto the bus. She was crouched with her back to him. She looked like she might be sick.

Without thinking, Sylvia reached out and scooped up the big-eared puppy. She acted quickly and the pup did not dart. Maybe he didn't have time to run from her. Maybe he was in shock. Before she could second-guess her actions, she stuffed the tiny dog under her oversized sweatshirt and looked at Xander like she'd just swallowed a goldfish.

It took Xander a moment to realize what was happening—that his girlfriend had a dog under her sweatshirt. "What are you doing?" he whispered in alarm. His eyes were as wide as hers. "You can't take that dog on the bus. You heard what he said. He thinks these strays are trash!"

"Well, then I guess I'm just picking up trash on the side of the road," Sylvia retorted, shrugging and trying to look calm. Xander clamped his mouth shut.

Sylvia gave a quick sweep of the area with her eyes but didn't see any other signs of puppy life. With her chin high and shoulders squared, she climbed back on the bus with a skinny and trembling Chihuahua mutt clutched tightly to her belly.

03

"You just picked him up? On the side of the road?" Sylvia's aunt Orelia, her mother's older sister, held the door to the small house open wide to welcome her niece and her boyfriend . . . and, apparently, a mangy mongrel. As her niece explained why she was holding the tiny mutt wrapped in her sweatshirt, Orelia's smile grew even wider and finally turned into a laugh. "You are just like Pedro." She chortled, motioning Xander, Sylvia, and her minuscule bundle through the door. Standing in the front hall, Orelia looked from her niece to her husband, Hector. "Isn't she just like your brother?" she asked with a raised eyebrow. "Pedro is always showing up with some pathetic creature that needs rescuing."

"It's true," Hector agreed, starting to chuckle himself. "And not just dogs."

Sylvia cradled the black-and-white puppy protectively. The little guy was in bad shape and almost completely hidden in the folds of her clothing. And while it was true that she wanted to help him (and admittedly every dog like him), she wasn't crazy. Nor was she crazy about being laughed at. The look on the dog's face suggested he wasn't too happy about it, either.

"Sylvia, honey, don't worry! It's a *good* thing," Orelia said when she noticed her niece bristling. "Pedro is amazing. He's made a career out of rescue dogs." She put her arm around Sylvia's shoulder and pulled her into the cozy, colorful kitchen.

Sylvia smiled and leaned into her aunt. She nodded. She got it. It was a compliment, not a joke. She remembered hearing about her uncle's brother, Pedro. He lived on a ranch in California that trained handlers and dogs to work together to save people after disasters. He was basically a hero.

Orelia and Hector welcomed Xander, shaking his hand and inviting him to take a seat at the table. "Would you like some coffee?" Hector asked.

Xander and Sylvia both accepted the offer, and while Hector poured the steaming dark liquid into mugs, Sylvia slowly unwrapped the bundle causing the commotion.

"Tía, Tío, this is Dusty," Sylvia said, introducing the puppy to her aunt and uncle. The scraggly puppy shivered in Sylvia's lap but held his head high. His ears dwarfed the rest of his body, which made him look even smaller than he was. His large eyes were runny, and his body was dotted with raw-looking bald patches. Still, the mix of Chihuahua and who-knows-what held his head up proudly.

"Dusty," Sylvia's uncle repeated. He shook his head, chuckling as he set the coffee and a carton of milk on the table.

"Thanks." Sylvia smiled. The name had been obvious from the moment she plucked him from the dusty, garbage-strewn roadside. She put her face close to the little dog's ear. "Nobody's gonna throw you away ever again," she crooned.

Xander's eyebrows went up, and he looked from his girlfriend to her family and back to his girlfriend. He hadn't been able to say anything to Sylvia on the bus, but now that they'd arrived at her aunt and uncle's there were some realities he and Sylvia needed to discuss. He hesitated, considering his words, and then spoke. "Sylvia, you know we can't take a puppy back to the States with us, right?" he said quietly. "I mean, even if we could get him cleared to get on the plane, dogs aren't allowed in our apartment."

Sylvia felt her heart sink at the reality of his words. Xander was right. She didn't like it, but he was right.

"I'm not sure what you were thinking," he added gently.

Orelia pulled teaspoons from a drawer and placed them on the table next to the mugs of coffee, which were growing cold. Normally she would say as much, but she knew better than to interrupt.

"I wasn't thinking," Sylvia admitted. "Or at least I wasn't thinking things through." She'd half realized this at the time, but it hadn't mattered. She'd been faced with a decision—to let the pup die or to help him live, and she'd done what she thought was right. She saved the Chihuahua from living alone next to a highway, from being run over like the rest of his family, from starving. But now, sitting in her aunt's kitchen, the reality of what she had taken on was hitting her. Hard. By snatching up this puppy and carrying him onto the bus, she had committed herself to finding him a decent life. She couldn't just put him back down somewhere. She'd made a kind of promise. "But how could I leave him?" she asked softly.

Using two fingers so she wouldn't overwhelm his little body, Sylvia gave Dusty a slow pet from the crown of his head to the base of his wispy tail. He warmed to her touch, leaning into it. Orelia, Hector, and Xander all watched, all saw the connection between them. Sylvia had fallen hard for Dusty, and the feeling seemed to be mutual. Sylvia gazed down at the pup, not seeing his inflamed skin, protruding ribs, or scabby paws. She put her head close to his and whispered something the other humans couldn't hear.

Xander watched his softhearted, animal-loving girlfriend and bit his bottom lip. "I'm not sure the little guy will survive until we get home, anyway," he whispered softly. Orelia and Hector nodded in solemn agreement.

Dusty could not stop shaking, even in Sylvia's hands. He looked around the small room. It was filled with smells of food and people—four people, and they were all looking right at him. He felt exposed, and his eyes darted here and there, looking for a way out. He thought he should run. He thought he should hide. Then he felt Sylvia's gentle hand again as she ran her fingers over his head and down his back. All of a sudden he thought he should stay.

There was something about this young woman, these people. They felt different. They were not going to hurt him. Besides, he had nowhere to go. His family was gone. He was sick. He was weak. He was hurting. He didn't have the strength to get away, even if he'd had the opportunity.

Dusty (that's what she called him) looked up through his blurry eyes at the dark-haired woman petting him and wondered what would happen next. He put his nose in the air, noticing how much better it smelled here than near the trash heaps where he searched for supper. His stomach rumbled.

Sylvia set Dusty down on the floor, and the pup did the only thing he knew how to do: He started to sniff for food.

The people looked on. "You won't find much here, little dog. I just cleaned up," Orelia said in Spanish.

Dusty ignored her, nose down. He slipped between the counter and the stove, disappearing in the dark crack. A moment later he meandered out chewing a dried tortilla strip. The people laughed. "Are you trying to insult me, poquito?" Orelia asked. "Or do you just have a really good nose?" She trailed off, her eyes sparkling as she got some rice out of the fridge and served up a bowl with a little milk mixed in. She set it on the floor for Dusty, who dove in the moment his tortilla was gone.

Orelia watched him eat. She sat down beside her niece, eyes still sparkling. She had an idea, and the more she thought about it, the more she liked it.

"Thanks for seeing us!" Sylvia walked into the examination room at Milagros Caninos. The shelter was not far from her aunt and uncle's house, and specialized in fixing and caring for abandoned dogs. They treated sick animals and also helped with adoptions.

"It's not a problem. We've definitely done this before." A vet with light brown hair, an easy smile, and a stethoscope around his neck peered closely at Dusty.

Dusty, who had been getting bolder with each day in Sylvia's company, felt unsure and a little wobbly standing on a slick metal table. He was not crazy about this place. It smelled like disinfectant and had the faint whiff of panic.

"Tourists fall in love with the strays and want to take them home all the time," the vet went on. "All this puppy needs to board a plane with you is proof of a rabies vaccine and a certificate stating he's in good health."

Sylvia let out her breath. That sounded easy . . . except maybe the "good health" part. "So, no communicable diseases?" she asked hopefully. Malnutrition and scabby paws looked (and must have felt) terrible, but they weren't catching.

"Right. When is your flight?" he asked.

"In a week," Sylvia told him. The vet nodded. He reached for Dusty, who shrank away from him, ears down. The street dog was getting comfortable with Sylvia and her family, but was still wary of other people—especially men. Sylvia stroked his back and crooned, "It's okay. He just wants to help."

Dusty looked from Sylvia to the man and back. Slowly his ears stood back up. He understood that Sylvia thought the man was okay. Reluctantly he let the vet hold him, poke him, and turn him over. He kept his teeth together and fought the strong urge to nip the big stranger's pushy fingers.

"A week should be long enough for the mange to clear up. Keep him on puppy food, and I'll give you some drops for his eyes. He should be healthy enough before you go. But you're going to need a carrier."

The vet handed Dusty back to Sylvia. Xander raised his eyebrows. "Can't she just put him in her pocket?"

he joked. It was true that he would fit—Dusty was barely larger than two fists. The vet smiled but shook his head. "Airline regulations," he explained. "But don't worry, pup, you'll be in your new home before you know it!"

Sylvia didn't bother to explain that she wasn't going to be the one to adopt the little guy. They had other plans for him. Big plans. She lifted Dusty closer to her face, oblivious to his mangy skin. "You hear that?" She grinned. Of course he had, with those ears, but he hadn't understood. "You are about to fly off on a real adventure," she told him.

04

The days passed confusedly at Hector and Orelia's. Dusty slept a lot, but every time he awoke he was alarmed and leaped to his feet, forgetting where he was . . . forgetting that he was safe.

"It's okay, Dustito," Sylvia would usually croon from the sofa. Her words calmed him.

Food was another issue. Meals were provided twice a day, so Dusty never had to hunt for food. But he didn't know anything else and didn't know what to do with himself! Also, now that the food was plentiful, eating was hard. His system wasn't used to it. Digesting food took a lot of energy and was tricky at best. Sometimes it came back up, which was uncomfortable. Other times it sped through him too fast. It was out of his control. It was embarrassing. And a lot of the time it hurt.

Sylvia woke him up before sunrise on his last day in Mexico. When he staggered to his feet he saw that his bowl was gone. "Sorry, no breakfast for you. You don't want to get sick while we're traveling."

Dusty shook, his ears flapping, and then let Sylvia coax him into a soft-sided dog carrier. It was the smallest size they made and had mesh windows on the front and back.

It felt strange to be carried. Dusty tried standing but slid into the fabric walls whenever Sylvia walked. Finally he lay down. The jostling was more manageable that way. After a ride on a bus and an escalator and a moving sidewalk, they boarded another big vehicle with lots of small windows. Dusty could smell fuel and food and lots of people. It was like a bus, with rows of seats, but also different.

"Sorry you have to ride under here," Sylvia apologized as she pushed the carrier into a dark space beneath the seat in front of hers. Dusty looked out.

All he could see were purses, small bags, and feet. He heard voices. A rumbling engine. Dings. A muffled voice coming through speakers. He trembled in the dim tight quarters. If everything weren't so big, loud, new, and frightening, he could settle down. He liked small spaces. And he *used* to like the dark. Now it reminded him of the night not so long ago when he lost his pack. The dark had become something big and awful that swallowed his whole family in an instant.

Dusty let his tongue flop out of his mouth. He panted. He listened to Sylvia and Xander talk. The sounds of their voices and the thrum of engines finally helped him drift off to sleep.

"You're going to like it in California," Sylvia said. Her words roused Dusty, and he opened his eyes. She was leaning down so he could hear her clearly. She reached a hand in through the carrier door to give him a reassuring pat. "We're about to land." Dusty couldn't understand the words, but he read Sylvia's tone loud and clear. "Things are going to be okay," it said. Her voice was soothing, like the feel of his mother's tongue on the top of his head.

Dusty didn't shake even a little when the plane bumped down on the tarmac in San Francisco.

"We're most of the way there now!" Sylvia said. She pulled the carrier into her lap. "It's a good thing I still have a few more days before school starts," she said. Dusty wasn't sure whether she was talking to him or to Xander. He cocked his head to one side, lifting an ear.

Sylvia grinned. She hadn't thought it was possible, but Dusty was getting cuter by the second. After only ten days (and in spite of still being sick) he was heavier and healthier, too—which was a good thing. Her stomach did a flip. Dusty needed to be irresistible when they arrived at the Sterling Center. If the rescue dog operation turned him away, she wasn't sure what she'd do. Not that she was looking forward to leaving the little guy there. She held up the carrier so she could see how Dusty was doing.

"We can't keep him," Xander reminded her for the seventy-seventh time. Sylvia nodded sadly. She knew.

A few hours later, Sylvia, Xander, and Dusty pulled

into the parking lot in front of the Sterling Center. Dusty had traveled the whole last leg of the trip standing in Sylvia's lap with his nose lifted toward the crack in the passenger side window. Never before had he smelled so much so fast! He wanted to breathe in everything!

"Okay, little dude. Let's hope this goes well!" Sylvia would have crossed her fingers if she weren't holding Dusty. Yes, Orelia and Hector had called and told Pedro they were coming with a dog. But Sylvia knew for a fact that they hadn't gone into much detail.

The Sterling Center wasn't like the shelter they'd visited in Mexico. It was unique, and so were the canines who resided there. The dogs at Sterling were rescues, like Dusty, but instead of being adopted out to regular families they were trained to become search and rescue dogs, and then partnered with human handlers. The Sterlings trained human-canine teams to rescue people!

"I think that place rescued Pedro, too," Hector had explained. "My brother had a hard time settling down in his twenties and thirties, so he left Mexico.

He traveled all over. He only found his real home, and his real calling, when he started working for the Sterling Center."

Carrying Dusty to the door, Sylvia hoped this was the place that would help Dusty find his real home and calling. She heard the jangle of a bell overhead as they stepped into the welcome center. She paused, noticing a mass of shelves covered with books about dogs and dog training along one wall. Across from the shelves was another wall covered in awards and plaques and pictures of dogs. Sylvia blinked and felt her heart leap into her throat. All of the dogs in the photos were BIG.

"Hi," Sylvia said. The girl behind the desk couldn't have been older than fifteen. She tucked her pink-streaked hair behind her ears and gave the new arrivals her best "greeting the public" smile.

"Hello! Welcome to the Sterling Center. How can I help you?" Shelby Sterling asked. She *was* young and *very* professional. Most of the time. The second she spotted Dusty in Sylvia's arms, though, her professionalism flew right out the window. "Oh. My. Gosh.

Is that a *dog*?" she squeaked, coming around the desk for a closer look.

"This is Dusty," Sylvia said a little proudly.

"He's adorable!" the girl cooed. "Did you say he's named *Dusty*?"

"He was hiding on a dusty, trash-filled roadside when I found him," Sylvia explained with a grin.

Shelby stepped right up to the tiny pup, who didn't shy away from the attention as the young girl praised and pet him and now completely ignoring the woman holding him, as well as Xander. It was as if the humans had completely disappeared.

"So, do we need to sign him in or anything?" Xander finally asked a little awkwardly.

Shelby raised her head, appearing even more confused than she'd been about Dusty's name. "Sign him in?"

"Yes, um, we thought you were expecting him," Sylvia sputtered. "My aunt Orelia called from Mexico several days ago and talked to Pedro . . ."

"Oh," Shelby said, her eyebrows rising in surprise. "Oh!" she repeated when she grasped the misunderstanding. "Orelia . . . as in Pedro's sister-in-law? Your aunt? Of course he told me there was a new dog arriving . . . but . . . *this* is the dog?" she asked, her eyes glancing down at the minuscule pup. "I thought you were bringing a trainee. Dusty's . . . tiny!"

Xander looked at the floor. Sylvia bit her lip. Shelby blinked. It was true. Dusty did not look a thing like the certified search and rescue dogs on the wall. He did not look like a trainee.

The room went silent and Dusty felt six eyes fall on him. He returned the stares, leaned into the hand caressing him, and let out a decisive yap. He wasn't sure what these people were saying, but it didn't matter. He liked this place and had an announcement to make: He had arrived!

05

Now that he had everyone's attention, Dusty let out several more barks to make sure the humans got the message. "Yip! Yip, yip, yip!" He liked it here! This place was filled with light and air and really, really good smells . . . not the faintest whiff of rubber or garbage or gasoline. ¡Ninguno! His nostrils were gloriously jammed with people and dogs and treats and dirt.

"I'm Sylvia." Sylvia extended a hand to the young girl. "Pedro's niece."

Shelby flushed with embarrassment. "Oh, I'm so sorry!" she exclaimed, shaking Sylvia's hand. "I forgot to introduce myself. I'm Shelby." There was an awkward pause, and then she added, "It's not usually this quiet around here. My entire family is at the autumn potluck at the fire station in town."

Sylvia repositioned Dusty in the crook of her arm, realizing that she'd like to be at a potluck right now herself. It had been a busy day of travel, with inedible airplane food and little additional time to eat. "And my uncle?"

Shelby let out a laugh. "He's there, too. The dessert buffet is legendary . . . He talks about it all summer long and wonders why he has to eat dinner before he can dive in."

Sylvia's lips rose into a knowing smile. The Sundal sweet tooth was well established and documented. Her uncle Hector would take a side of sugar at every meal if her aunt Orelia allowed it. Needless to say, she didn't.

Shelby reached her hands out gently. "May I?" she asked, her eyes resettling on Dusty.

Sylvia hesitated. Dusty had been rescued just over a week before and was still getting used to being handled by new people. But he extended his neck to

Shelby and even licked her hand. It looked like he was fine with it! He allowed Sylvia to pass him over, and the little Chihuahua gazed intently into the teen-ager's eyes.

Shelby gazed right back. Dusty had a black face with an upside-down wishbone of white that settled on either side of his nose, and a body that was mostly white now that his hair was growing back. But more than anything, Dusty had *ears*—big, triangle-shaped ears that pointed up and out on either side of his sweet face. His ears were literally as tall as he was! They reminded Shelby of satellite dishes, and she sus-pected they picked up even the tiniest of sounds. His left ear looked like someone had taken a bite out of the tip, though it had healed up nicely for a dog who'd been living on the street. Shelby felt certain it made him even more adorable than he would have been without it.

"Yip, yip!" Dusty let out a double bark and wrig-gled in Shelby's arms. He was done being examined by this new person, who smelled like shampoo and enchiladas.

After getting an okay nod from Sylvia, Shelby set the little pup on the floor of the welcome center.

Dusty's tail wagged as he trotted over to the desk where the girl was sitting when he had come in. The floor was smooth and shiny under his paws, which were still burned and sore from the brutality of living on the street. His tummy rumbled. After more than a week of regular meals, his stomach was still uncomfortable most of the time, either gnawing with hunger or churning painfully in an effort to digest food. But no matter what it was doing, Dusty's instinct told him to do one thing and one thing only: find food. He made a beeline for a tall plastic container with tangy delicious smells inside. He lifted himself onto his back paws and stretched upward, but his front paws were still several inches from the top. He let out a frustrated yip before remembering that, like always, there was another way. He knew what to do!

While the humans talked, Dusty backed up until he stood several feet away from the plastic box. He tightened his muscles and took off at a dead run, heading straight for it. He threw his body with full force against the bin. ¡Ay, Chihuahua!

The garbage can fell over onto its side, making the people turn in time to see a slightly dazed Dusty getting to his feet and shaking off the tumble. It was worth it. With the recycling bin on its side, he had full access to the not-yet-rinsed yogurt container he'd smelled. While Sylvia and the others laughed, he got to work licking up every remaining tidbit of tang.

"We've been feeding him, I swear," Sylvia said. "Twice a day!"

Shelby nodded. "We see that a lot with dogs who have suffered from hunger. Their bodies take a long time to forget what it was like to never have enough to eat. Some never do . . ."

She watched the pup work, using his tiny tongue to clean out every millimeter of the plastic container. "Has he shown any aggression around food?"

Sylvia shook her head no. "None at all."

Shelby smiled. "That's a good sign. Sometimes we have dogs who—"

A bell jangled and the threesome turned to see a gaggle of people traipsing through the front door.

"Sylvia!" a man cried, rushing up to her with arms wide.

Sylvia didn't actually recognize her uncle Pedro—she hadn't seen him since she was just a child. But his resemblance to Hector was undeniable, from his twinkly brown eyes to his close-cut, salt-and-pepper hair. They even had the same goatee!

"¡Tío!" she replied as they hugged. Pedro's embrace was strong and welcoming, and Sylvia had the sense that no matter how unusual or unorthodox Dusty may be, she'd brought him to the right place. Pedro released her and stood back, smiling.

"This is my boyfriend, Xander," Sylvia said, introducing him to Pedro.

"Are you a nice boyfriend?" asked a voice. The youngest girl in the group stood right next to Xander holding a very large tabby cat and scowling up at him.

"Juniper!" a woman, presumably her mother, scolded.

The other Sterling kids, who definitely looked related, with their wide-set eyes and delicate features, rolled their eyes. Shelby tugged her little sister's twisted braid.

Pedro chuckled. "Sylvia, Xander, this is Juniper," he said. "And her friend there is Twig."

"He's not my friend—he's my soul mate!" Juniper corrected. She looked around, as if making sure the coast was clear, and then leaned in close to Sylvia and Xander. "He's also the best cat in the universe, but don't tell Bud I said that. He's very sensitive because he lost his mother so young."

"That's a whole other story, June Bug," a tall man with light eyes like the boy's replied. He smiled as he rested a gentle hand on the little girl's shoulder.

"Nice to meet you, Juniper, Twig," Sylvia said. She considered shaking the cat's paw, but then thought better of it—he looked like he'd been eating lemons.

"And now for the rest of the Sterlings." Pedro waved an arm in the direction of the small crowd. "This is Frances, our illustrious founder and visionary," he began, and then took them through a flurry of names and introductions. Roxanne, tall, thin, and imposing, was the lead dog trainer. Frances's son Martin, the man standing with Juniper, was in charge of maintenance and facilities. His wife, Georgia, was, according to Pedro, basically in charge of everything else. Sylvia believed it—Georgia had a firm handshake and seemed both no-nonsense and competent.

The two kids they hadn't met were Forrest and Morgan. Forrest was the only boy in the family, and Morgan seemed the opposite of Juniper . . . shy and quiet.

"We will have a quiz in the morning," Pedro joked.

Sylvia shook her head in protest. "Sorry, Tío, no can do. Xander and I are still on summer break! Plus, we have to make the drive back to school tonight."

Everyone was chuckling when Forrest suddenly blurted, "Hey, where's the new recruit?" The entire crowd looked around the room for the dog they knew Sylvia had brought but they hadn't seen, and Sylvia herself was shocked that she'd forgotten about Dusty for the last several minutes. Shelby, though, had slipped behind the desk, where she suspected there were drips of enchilada sauce left from her dinner. She tenderly scooped the dog up and carried him over to her eagerly awaiting family.

"Everyone, this is Dusty," she announced.

Nine pairs of eyes landed on the Chihuahua mix, and eight jaws dropped open (Twig just yawned).

"That's the dog you brought from Mexico?" Pedro asked, clearly shocked.

"Yes," Sylvia replied as worry swept over her. She knew he was small but hadn't expected a group of dog people to respond so . . . negatively. After all, he *was* a dog.

Pedro ran a hand through his graying hair. "Hector said he was a street mutt, but all they talked about was his incredible nose. They didn't mention that he was, he was so . . . so . . ."

"Ratlike!" Forrest guffawed.

"He could be stunted because of malnutrition," Sylvia said, feeling both defensive and alarmed.

"How much does he weigh?" Morgan, the quiet girl, asked.

"Six pounds," Sylvia replied.

"He looks like a mix of miniature Italian Greyhound

and Chihuahua," Roxanne commented.

"With a little flying squirrel thrown in . . ." Forrest added with laugh.

"Yip!" Dusty barked in protest.

"I think he's perfect," Shelby said.

Cocoa, Frances's elderly chocolate Lab, sniffed her way up to Dusty. Dusty's tail went into overdrive, while Cocoa's swayed leisurely from side to side.

"He's not even as big as Cocoa's head!" Juniper half shouted. "He's smaller than Twig!" She squeezed the hefty orange tabby cat in her arms, and Sylvia realized that the cat was completely ignoring *both* dogs.

Frances's gaze rested curiously on the puppy in Shelby's arms. "We don't usually do DNA tests on the dogs," she mused, "but I bet this little critter would yield some interesting results."

Roxanne nodded—no one could argue with that! Dusty was definitely an unusual mix of breeds.

Sylvia was relieved that the mood in the room had seemed to lighten . . . until she turned back toward her uncle. His initial smile for his niece had completely disappeared, leaving a very concerned frown in its place.

Pedro could not take his eyes off the dog. The question in his mind was not "What is he?" but "What am I going to do with him?" Pedro's work on the ranch kept him busy all the time. It was his job to connect with people who wanted to know more about or pair with search and rescue dogs, and it seemed as though there were more of them every day! He almost always had a small crew of humans in training on the ranch and was constantly updating his curriculum to keep it fresh. He'd assumed that Dusty would become a canine trainee and be handed off to Roxanne almost immediately but could now see the truth. Dusty was no rescue dog. He was a teensy-tiny mongrel.

And as of right this minute he was also one hundred percent Pedro's responsibility.

06

"Let's bring this little guy out to my trailer, and I can show you the ranch on the way," Pedro said, trying to sound upbeat. He could tell by Sylvia's furrowed brow and worried eyes that she saw his reservation about Dusty, and he didn't want her to feel bad. It wasn't she who'd told him about the dog or conveniently left out the details regarding his size. That would be his brother, Hector. Sylvia was just a person who needed help with a dog, a dog she couldn't help but assist on the side of the road. And though Pedro couldn't deny feeling a bit over a barrel—canine "pets" other than Cocoa weren't allowed on the ranch, and he didn't really have time for a dog, anyway—he had agreed to take on the dog over the phone and at the very least needed to find him a home.

"Great," Xander said, speaking for both of them. Shelby handed Dusty to Sylvia, and the Sterling kids clamored to come, too—all except Shelby, who still had to answer the welcome center phones. Pedro led everyone out the back door amid chatter and Georgia's reminders about chores and bedtime.

Back in Sylvia's arms, Dusty sat up straight, his ears pricking with the sounds of the ranch. The sun was low on the horizon, and birds were chirping as they winged their way across the inky pink sky. And the smells! Earth, grasses, sage, people, and dogs. Dogs, dogs, dogs! Dusty's nose quivered. Somewhere nearby there were a *lot* of dogs.

"I live out on the edge of the property," Pedro explained, "so we can show you everything between here and there." He pointed to a large gray building in front of them. "That's my work territory," he said. "The handlers' lodge. It's where the folks who come here to learn how to be dog handlers live, as well as where they do their classroom training." He paused, then added, "The goal is for each of them to become trained enough to be paired with a dog . . . hopefully the right one."

"Pedro has the hardest job of all," Forrest explained, his eyes alight. "Training the humans!"

They kept walking, passing a small wood-shingled house on the left. "That's where my grandmother lives with Cocoa," Juniper announced. She was still carrying the tabby, and Sylvia was amazed that the cat still wasn't reacting to Dusty. It was as if the little Chihuahua were invisible. Dusty, for his part, seemed too busy checking out this new place to care much about the cat, either.

"When Grandma first started the center it was just her and one dog, but now it's huge!" Forrest crowed gleefully.

Sylvia nodded in agreement, sensing the pride the Sterling kids had in the ranch. Sylvia could see why. The Sterling Center was an incredible place doing incredible work.

"As of last month the center has successfully trained forty-eight teams for SAR certification,"

Morgan informed everyone. "Did you know a trained search and rescue dog can do the search work of thirty humans? They can cover more ground and safely go places people can't. We estimate that the Sterling dogs have saved over thirty-five lives."

"That's amazing," Xander said. He'd heard about SAR dogs, but hadn't really understood how essential their work was during rescue efforts. He hadn't known that they saved so many people.

"Totally," Sylvia agreed.

"Yip!" Dusty agreed, too.

"This is where Roxanne runs the dogs through their training paces before they get into more advanced practice and terrain," Pedro said as the group passed through a relatively open area with low shrubs, a covered training arena with balance beams, ladders, barrels and tubes, and a shade structure with seating. A small trailer fitted with a giant window stood at the edge of the space.

"That's the observation trailer," Forrest explained. "So we can watch what's going on with the dogs in training without disturbing the process."

The group kept walking and soon came across a giant woodpile. Pedro steered them toward a large building in the distance, and Sylvia felt Dusty squirm in her arms, tail wagging.

"Yip!" he barked. "Yip, yip, yip!" The smell of dog was getting stronger with every step, and within a couple of minutes they were inside the canine pavilion, which as far as Dusty could tell was a doggy *castle*. His nose and tail were both on overdrive, quivering with excitement. They strolled past the kennels, where the dogs lounged happily on their beds or trotted up to the doors to say hello.

"This is where I work," Forrest said, waving an arm grandly. "And sometimes Morgan, too. The dogs need a lot of care between feeding and grooming and watering and exercising," he said. "They're like elite athletes, and we're their entourage."

Dusty's tail was wagging like mad, and his eyes were bright. The whole ranch smelled good, but this place smelled like bowls of kibble and lots of dogs, and he could see soft beds where pups were dozing. It looked and smelled like happiness—like doggy heaven—and he was sad when Sylvia followed the man back outside. He wanted to stay in there forever!

Forrest jogged ahead toward a massive pile of debris. "This is our rubble pile!" he said. "It's meant to be like a collapsed building after a disaster. It looks accidental, but my dad spends a lot of time with a skid loader making this thing as close to the real thing as possible so the dogs can really learn how to search."

Sylvia shuddered as she imagined people trapped under the enormous pile in front of her—it was easily the size of a football field. Twisted pipes, chunks of concrete, rebar, steel beams, splintered wood . . . it was literally a disaster zone. She instinctively squeezed Dusty in a hug, suddenly glad he would never have to climb on or in the hazardous pile.

"Don't worry, I'm going to find a good home for Dusty," Pedro said, as if reading her thoughts. "A nice family for him to live with."

Sylvia swallowed and nodded. That sounded terrific.

"Okay, kids, thanks for your tour guide assistance," Pedro said. "I can take it from here."

Juniper let out a groan of disappointment. "It's not even dark yet!" she complained.

"You heard Mom," Morgan said, putting a hand on Juniper's shoulder. She quickly shrugged it off but turned to follow her older brother and sister down the path to their house. All of them knew better than to test their mother.

The three kids gave a final wave goodbye, and Pedro led Xander, Sylvia, and Dusty toward his little trailer at the edge of the ranch. On the way they paused briefly at the newest addition to the training center, a recently donated bus. The wrecked vehicle lay on its side as if it had been totaled in a crash.

"We are always increasing our facilities," Pedro explained. "We want our dogs to experience as many possible scenarios before they leave here, because it helps lessen on-the-job trauma and gives them better success rates in the field. This bus was in an accident about a month ago and was donated last week."

The huge vehicle lay near the edge of a wooded

area littered with giant boulders. Dusty's body stilled and he stifled a whimper when it came into view. Sylvia's hand flew to her mouth.

"Oh!" she exclaimed.

There were no glaring headlights, but it was a stark reminder of the bus that claimed Dusty's pack.

The small dog whined, which Pedro hadn't heard before. Up until now he'd seemed happy. "Was he in a bus crash?" he asked quietly.

"Not exactly," Xander explained. "Sylvia and I were on the bus that killed Dusty's family. Sylvia found him in the gutter right afterward. She snatched him up and snuck him onto the bus."

Pedro instinctively reached out a hand and stroked Dusty's soft head, recommitting to the tiny pup. He was a lucky dog, and Pedro hoped he could keep the luck going, even if Dusty couldn't stay on the ranch.

Sylvia sensed what Pedro was thinking and her heart warmed. She gave Dusty a kiss behind the ear. "Don't worry," she whispered. "You will be safe here."

Fifty or so yards away, at the top of a crested hill surrounded by scrub pine, stood Pedro's trailer. Pedro held the door wide open. Inside, the small home was cozy vintage, with dark wood cabinets, linoleum floor tile, a colorful patterned rug, and comfy furniture in the living room. The bedroom was small but had a window that overlooked the ranch.

"It's not much, but it's all mine," Pedro said from the kitchen. He filled a bowl with fresh water and set it on the floor for Dusty, who thirstily lapped it up. "Ours," he added. "For now."

Sylvia's heart squeezed as she watched the dog drink. She didn't want to leave him, but it was time for her and Xander to go. They had to get to school and this stop hadn't been on their original schedule. After Dusty drank his fill, she picked him up one last time.

"We have to take off, little guy," she said. He felt her reluctance. His triangle ears drooped as he remembered the *first* time she picked him up—out of the ditch on the side of the dark road. He remembered the yelling bus driver and his mama and sisters lying still on the pavement. He remembered how sad he was, how hungry and scared. Sylvia had held him close in her sweatshirt, hiding him from the bus driver. Protecting him.

With his ears still low, Dusty extended his neck and licked her face again and again, each lick a thank-you. He knew she had saved him. Once by bringing him onto the bus. And twice by bringing him to this good place.

Sylvia wiped a tear from her cheek. "You're going to be okay, Dustito," she whispered, her nose touching the soft fur of his muzzle. "My uncle will find you a wonderful home."

"You can find your way back to your car?" Pedro asked.

Xander and Sylvia nodded yes in unison.

Pedro took Dusty into his own arms—or hands, since the pup was so tiny—and together they stood on the porch and watched Sylvia and Xander walk past the bus wreck and beyond the canine pavilion. Pedro could feel Dusty's ribs so easily he could have played him like a twelve-string guitar, and he held him as gently as possible. When Sylvia and Xander were moving specks in the fading light, the pair stepped back into the living room of the trailer.

It wasn't a forever home for Dusty, but for now it would have to do.

07

Pedro awoke the next morning with the sense that something was not quite right, and it took several seconds for him to realize that there was no pillow cradling his head. He opened his eyes and saw a tiny, black-and-white Chihuahua stretched out contentedly on his pillow, his back left paw just a few inches from Pedro's nostrils.

Rising up on an elbow, he inspected the burns and scabs on the pup's paw pads. A visit with a vet was today's first order of business. He watched as Dusty stretched and opened an eye, and then craned *his* cradled neck to give Pedro a lick.

"Good morning to you, too," Pedro replied with a

chuckle. The pup had gone to sleep on a folded-up blanket next to Pedro's bed, and he wondered how long he'd stayed there before deciding to make his way to higher ground. And then . . . how had he climbed up? Pedro's bed was a good twenty inches off the floor!

Dusty finished his greeting and gingerly got to his feet, stretching. "I guess it's a good thing you weigh next to nothing, walking around on those sore feet," Pedro said. "Sorry you had to survive on the street, little guy. But that doesn't change the fact that that's my pillow!" He snatched it gently out from under Dusty, who reluctantly leaped off the bed.

Dusty watched Pedro eat a bowl of cereal, his mouth watering. Drool pooled on the linoleum floor beneath his head. Pedro felt bad that he hadn't thought to bring some kibble up to his trailer. "You'll have your own breakfast soon," he promised. He drank the last bit of milk from the bowl and dropped it in the sink. As he turned to go, an unsavory smell wafted up to his nostrils. The tiny Chihuahua crouched directly over his slippers, his face a mask of concentration. Pedro heard a tiny, gassy explosion echo in the room. Dusty looked up at him with a mixture of relief and apology.

"Really?" Pedro said as he picked up the dog with one hand and the slipper with the other. The smell was worse up close.

"Really," he answered himself as he carried both outside and dropped the slipper near the door. They were running late and he'd have to deal with it later.

In the canine pavilion, Morgan and Forrest were already doing the regular morning dog care. Pedro set Dusty down and went to wash his hands.

"Hey, little rat," Forrest greeted with a smirk while Morgan got a bowl and put a small amount of kibble in it. She didn't think her brother was being kind, but wasn't sure how she felt about this new recruit . . . for the first time in ages she herself hadn't fallen in love with a dog the moment he or she arrived. It was an odd situation for sure.

While Dusty gobbled up his breakfast, Georgia arrived at the pavilion with Dr. Jessica, the on-call vet who came to the ranch on an as-needed basis.

"I figured our tiny guest would need an exam," Georgia said, her brown eyes traveling to the dog, who was busily licking every last speck of food from a bowl that was twice the size he was.

"Gracias, Georgia," Pedro replied. He still had the uneasy feeling that he was in a bit of a pickle—he didn't have the time or the energy to find a home for this little guy—but was keenly aware of the fact that having the ranch's resources at his fingertips was a blessing. Making sure Dusty was healthy and ready for adoption was a big step toward actually getting him adopted. "Good morning, Dr. Jess," he added.

Jessica's eyebrows shot up so high they nearly touched her hairline, showing her surprise as she appraised Dusty. "He's not exactly your typical rescue dog, is he?" she noted.

Forrest hooted loudly. "Dusty, a rescue dog? Now *that's* hilarious!"

"He's not a recruit," Georgia explained. "Pedro's niece brought him last night—she found him on the street in Mexico and thought we could help find him a home."

"It may as well have been right here in California," Dr. Jessica said. "We've had twenty dumped puppies come into the shelter in just the past two weeks." She sighed, feeling the weight of the battle. "I hope we can find homes for them as well."

Pedro lifted Dusty off the ground and followed Georgia and Dr. Jessica to a nearby exam room. Dr. Jess examined Dusty quickly and gently. She checked his heart and ears. She palpated his stomach and felt for his organs. She was gentler than the vet in Mexico, but Dusty's nose twitched just the same. The table was just as cold and just as slippery. It was hard to stand up! And it didn't smell good in here like it did in the big room of the puppy palace.

"Considering he's only been off the streets about a week, he's doing pretty well," she noted. "He doesn't have mange, worms, or fleas."

Pedro was glad to hear it, since they'd just shared a pillow.

"Still, he's not entirely out of the woods. He's definitely underweight, and based on my internal exam I suspect he's having digestive issues."

Pedro nodded grimly, remembering the state of his slipper. Dusty certainly was.

"His pads are also in bad shape—burned on the hot pavement, no doubt." She made some notes on a chart.

"He needs ointment put on his feet several times a day." She pulled a tube from her bag and slathered on a thick layer of the antibiotic.

Dusty didn't waste a second getting to work licking off the goo. Dr. Jess half laughed. "And he's going to need near-constant supervision. He should wear socks or booties so he doesn't lick obsessively and make his condition worse. The faster he can grow new tissue, the better." She handed the tube of ointment to Pedro, who was getting more worried by the moment. Caring for Dusty was going to be time-consuming . . . like a full-time job, which he already had!

Dr. Jess made a few more notes. "We need to get his stomach accustomed to dog food, which could take a while. Let's start him on some new food this afternoon, and give him four small meals a day for the first week. More than four would mean he'd have to spend a lot of time and energy digesting, but four won't feel constant and should keep his stomach from having to process too much kibble at one time. When he's adjusted we can drop to two daily meals and increase the amount."

"It's too bad we can't feed him garbage . . ." Pedro joked. "We know his stomach is accustomed to *that* . . ." But his smile faded quickly as Dr. Jessica handed the pup back to Pedro. He had a busy schedule on the ranch, one that didn't allow for him to be a twenty-four-hour dog sitter! Georgia eyed the dog and trainer pair, seeming more than a little concerned herself. The ranch was a busy place, and there were always trainers and dogs waiting. It wasn't as if Dusty was one of them!

Feeling slightly numb and being unusually silent, Pedro walked out of the exam room and nearly bumped into Shelby, who was lurking just outside the door.

"Aren't you supposed to be at the welcome center

desk?" Georgia asked, spotting her daughter and employee.

"Bathroom run," Shelby replied quickly. Georgia tipped her head knowingly and opened her mouth to point out that the bathroom was, as far as she knew, still in the opposite direction. But before she could get the words out she noticed that her eldest daughter was gazing at Dusty like he was the most handsome dog in the entire world and not the large-eared, puny, underweight mutt he actually was.

"Time to get back to work, Shelby," she said instead. "The welcome center needs to be staffed at all times."

"Grandma is covering for me. She was working in the office . . ." People who had heard about the center stopped by unannounced on a regular basis, and calls came in daily from fire and police departments looking to get trained dogs. Everything funneled through the welcome center. It was the face of the ranch.

Shelby's gaze still rested on the Chihuahua runt. With a sigh she prepared to tear herself away, but Dusty stretched his neck and licked her hand. It was all the encouragement Shelby needed.

"I could keep an eye on him for you," she said, looking at Pedro. Her mom might say no, but Pedro . . . "He can sit on my lap while I work, and I can do the ointment and keep him from licking and make sure he gets the new kibble four times a day."

Georgia raised an eyebrow. "Bathroom break, huh?"

"I was just worried. He's so little. And I missed him," Shelby admitted. "Morgan told me you guys had him with Dr. Jess and I just wanted to find out what was going on." She halted, but her hand rested lovingly on the dog's back. "Sorry, Mom."

Georgia considered the situation. She didn't want her daughter to be distracted—she had an important job to do, and work was work. But she couldn't ignore the hopeful expression on Pedro's face, or the fact that Shelby was offering a workable solution that could benefit all of them, Dusty included.

The decision was clear. "Okay, you can keep an eye on Dusty. But I still expect you to manage your responsibilities."

Pedro let out a relieved breath and handed Dusty over. "Gracias, Shelby," he said, smiling.

"Yip, yip!" Dusty barked before licking Shelby's face repeatedly. Georgia smiled, hard-pressed to be certain who was happiest about the arrangement—Pedro, Dusty, or Shelby!

08

"All of that came out of *you?*" Shelby stared at the big pile of puked-up kibble on the floor and the very small, very sorry-looking dog standing next to it. Normally she would not go near barf (because it made her want to, um, barf), but what choice did she have? She'd offered to take care of the dog. And besides, it was for Dusty.

Squatting down next to the mess with a handful of paper towels, she cleaned it up as quickly as she could. When she'd disposed of it in the outside trash, keeping it as far from her body as possible, she returned to pick up the kitten-sized dog.

"You do weigh less than Twig, don't you?" she

crooned in Dusty's ears. "But everyone knows he's a monster. Still, if you want to get bigger you have to keep the food inside a little longer." She couldn't quite believe how hard she'd fallen for this little guy. She'd only spent a few afternoons with him but already found herself dreaming of keeping him even though that was totally against Sterling rules. No pet dogs in the family household. Period.

"You might be more Bud-sized." Bud was the tiny gray-furred runt of a litter of kittens and the last pet allowed. The Sterlings had found him in the maintenance shed. Well, Morgan and a dog-in-training named Ember found him. They'd been on a secret search for Twig, who'd gone missing and whose absence was making Juniper even more impossible to live with than she usually was . . .

"Yes, I'd say you are just a teensy bit bigger than Bud, but way, way cuter! Maybe I can convince Mom you're more like a cat," she rambled, scratching him behind the ears. Dusty stopped licking his double-layered doggy socks for a second, his giant ears twitching. His nose sniffed the air and his black-spotted tongue re-emerged, this time to lick Shelby's cheek. She giggled.

"If you don't stop your licking, I'm going to have to put a third pair of booties on you, and you won't be able to walk!"

"Yip!" Dusty protested.

Shelby shook her head. "Doctor's orders," she said, wagging a finger. The single layer of fabric had proven completely worthless—Dusty had *plenty* of determination!—so Shelby had added a second pair. She'd had to scrounge around the cabinets in the pavilion to find a pair of baby socks and then stitch up the sides to make them narrow enough to stay on his skinny legs.

"Thank goodness the phones have been quiet today!" she told him. Between his licking obsession and keeping up with her friends, there wasn't a lot of time to field Sterling calls. "And that my homework load is light."

Dusty put his tiny black nose up to hers and Shelby's heart melted. Could there be a more adorable creature on the entire earth?

Ping! Her cell phone alerted her to a new DM. It was Alice, her longtime best friend.

Bunch of us going 2 movies tonite, and u-know-who is coming!

Shelby felt a little tingle of excitement. There was another extremely adorable creature on the horizon, and his name was Ryan Westerly. Ryan transferred into her school in the spring of freshman year. From the moment he'd taken a seat in her bio class Shelby was crushing, big-time. Friendly and just plain nice, Ryan had big, dark eyes and bangs pushed off his forehead in an adorable swoop. So far, this year in chem, she hadn't been able to tell if he liked her like *that* but spending time with him outside of science was the best way to find out.

She was about to type **I'm there!** when she remembered they had a family dinner—it was her grandmother's birthday. **I can't tonite**, she typed instead, feeling thoroughly disappointed.

The moment she hit send her little brother pushed

through the back door of the welcome center.

"I need your lap rat. It's time for his feeding. We'll handle his medicine in the canine pavilion, too," Forrest panted.

Shelby scowled.

"Mom told me to go ahead and treat him like a rescue trainee as long as he's living with Pedro." Forrest cracked up as the words "rescue" and "trainee" came out of his mouth. "As *if.* Can you imagine this rodent becoming a rescue dog? Freaking ridiculous! I bet they don't even make working vests that small!"

Shelby's mood soured and she pursed her bow lips at her brother. "Oh shut it, Forrest." She glanced at the computer screen in front of her. She was supposed to be posting adoption notices about Dusty but hadn't made much progress. Her heart just wasn't in it. The truth was, she was desperate to keep him, but the Sterlings had a rule: no dogs as pets. There were always multiple dogs on the ranch who needed care and attention and training . . . every single day. Adding pet canines to the mix would make more work and could be problematically distracting. Besides,

Georgia said, they all loved dogs so much that if they started adopting, they'd be overrun. So Shelby's parents held hard and fast to the no-dogs-as-pets rule.

"Oh, are you defending your new boyfriend?" Forrest teased.

"Dusty is not a rat!" Shelby snapped, though it was clear from the smirk on her brother's face that he was just trying to get a rise out of her. Forrest was closest to Shelby in age and generally more clueless but less irritating than her sisters. Not today!

Forrest backed down a little. "Just teasing, Shel."

"I'll have you know that Dusty has a great nose and is one of the most persistent pups I have ever seen," she defended. "As persistent as any of those big dogs in the pavilion."

Forrest laughed hard at that, nearly doubling over. Shelby could be dramatic but wasn't usually delusional. Who was she kidding?

Dusty let out a yip and turned his head away, pointing his butt in Forrest's direction to demonstrate exactly how he felt about being laughed at.

Scowling at Captain Annoying, Shelby reluctantly

handed the dog over. For the first time in ages she kind of wished she was back on dog care—usually a punishment in her mind—instead of working the front office. Then she could shove her annoying brother aside and take care of Dusty herself. "Be careful with his socks," Shelby said. "I sewed the sides to make them narrower, but they're still a little loose."

"You mean his foot diapers?"

Shelby looked like she was going to leap over the desk and punch her brother. Forrest knew it was time to head out, and pronto.

"Let's go, big guy," he said with a smirk. Dusty settled into his arms reluctantly, not understanding his sarcasm. He hadn't completely forgiven the boy for laughing, but he smelled like peanut butter, which trumped pretty much everything and prompted a lick.

"Not too much food," Shelby called after them. "He's still not keeping it down!"

Forrest grinned as he carried the dog away from his sister. "You've got a long tongue for a rat . . ." He chortled as the door swung closed behind him.

It was all Shelby could do not to throw something at his retreating back.

Dusty wagged like crazy as they neared the canine pavilion. There was something about the ranch and the people on it that made Dusty forget all about the humans who'd been cruel or indifferent—the people who treated dogs like trash. Here, dogs were treated well. Like treasures, or royalty. The doggy castle was proof of that. It was big. It was tidy. Besides the beds, water, and food, the palace was never too hot or too cold. Nobody yelled or kicked or used brooms as weapons. It felt happy. And safe.

The moment Forrest set Dusty down on the smooth floor, Dusty began his food-sniffing routine. He slipped a little on his sock booties but quickly adjusted his movements to stay steady. He knew he wouldn't find any food—the floor of the palace was spotless. He also knew a bowl of kibble was coming. Neither of these things altered his behavior, though. Hunting for food was deeply ingrained. His tail on high, he sniffed and searched.

"He moves on those sock things pretty well,"

Forrest commented as he readied the leashes for the post-breakfast potty walks the dogs always got. "He's an agile little rat!"

Dusty was too busy investigating an alluring smell that was wafting out of the recycling bin to pay attention to the humans . . . until Morgan, the girl who'd been feeding him, called him over. She was crouched low with a miniature metal bowl—borrowed from Twig—ready. Dusty sat on his haunches and gazed up at her unbelievingly. Even after days and days of being served regular meals, he felt happy and surprised every time.

"Good sit," Morgan praised as she set the bowl in front of him. She watched Dusty dig in, gobbling the food without really chewing. "Hey, slow down!" she advised, like always. "We want it to stay in!"

Dusty heard the words but didn't slow down. It was sooooooo good! Lately Morgan had been putting something soft and wet in the bowl along with the dry bits. It didn't taste like much, but it made the kibble a little chewy. And though Dusty had learned that kibble could come out in ways that didn't feel good at all, that would happen later. Right now it was going in, and that was *always* delicious!

"I don't even know how he does that," Forrest commented as he watched Dusty inhale the last of the bowl. "It's like he's not even breathing!"

"I know," Morgan said. "He eats faster than any dog I've ever seen. But his stools have been a tiny bit firmer lately, so that's good."

"Do you think it's the pumpkin?" Forrest asked.

Morgan nodded. "It has a lot of fiber and will help with digestion. Kind of like a stomach buffer. And it doesn't have any of the side effects anti-diarrheal pharmaceuticals do."

Forrest shook his close-cropped head at his sister, his eyes rolling back in disgust. "Did you just say 'anti-diarrheal pharmaceuticals'?" He didn't mind cleaning up after the dogs, but words like that made him shudder.

"Yes," Morgan answered earnestly. "Diarrhea in dogs can be life-threatening—especially in malnourished dogs who don't have reserves."

"Right," Forrest replied, ready for this conversation

to be over. His younger sister talked like a professor. He snatched up the leashes and went to get two dogs-in-training to walk with Dusty. The elimination area was large and often changing... the pit stop got smelly fast. Forrest bagged all the poop, but it still reeked of dog pee, even after it had been hosed down.

Dusty trotted right over to a bush with yellowing leaves and lifted his tiny, sock-covered leg. With that matter handled, he moved on to find an acceptable spot to squat. Morgan joined the party but turned her head away when she saw Dusty. Dogs didn't like onlookers while doing their business, and who could blame them? She didn't, either! When she turned back to see the deposit, her lips parted into a wide smile. It was an actual pile!

"Awesome job, Dusty!" she cheered, pulling out a biodegradable poop bag. She picked up the load and tied it off.

Not too far away, Forrest was laughing again. "Who'd a thought we'd get this excited about poop?" he asked. "Way to go, lap rat!"

09

Pedro whistled tunelessly as he approached the welcome center doorway. Despite the nagging feeling that came from not having found Dusty a home, there was a lightness in his chest. The truth was, he looked forward to seeing the Chihuahua pup at the end of every day. Now that he was no longer pooping in his slippers or stealing his pillow, he really enjoyed Dusty's company. He appreciated his intelligence and the fact that he'd picked up obedience training so easily. And he admired his spunk—the tiny perro would *not* be pushed around. Pedro also liked waking up with the tiny ball of warmth next to his chest . . . maybe even loved it.

"How's it going in here?" he asked as the door jangled. Shelby beamed at him from the other side of the desk, while Morgan, who was looking over the center's shelves of books, waved a casual hello.

"Yip!" came Dusty's greeting. He hopped down off Shelby's lap and scampered, sock free, over to Pedro, his nails clicking on the linoleum. His pads were ninety percent healed. Lifting onto his back legs, he held remarkably steady and gave Pedro's hand a lick.

"Little dude can balance," Pedro noted.

"We weighed him this morning," Morgan reported. "He's gained three pounds!"

Pedro crouched and Dusty flopped over to let the bearded man scratch his belly—his new favorite treat. The two of them had discovered that Dusty liked a tummy scratch while watching TV together on Pedro's couch. Now he couldn't get enough.

"Well done, Dustito!" Pedro complimented.

"I wish he could stay with me." Shelby half pouted, watching the two of them. "We don't get enough time together on school days. He could stay the night . . . like a sleepover!"

Pedro stood and approached the desk. "No es posible," he said, feeling a little sad for Shelby. He hadn't told anyone that Dusty was sleeping in his bed with him. He actually felt kind of guilty about it, because he'd always thought dogs should be part of a family but not entitled to the same sleeping conditions as humans. Still, he obviously didn't feel guilty enough to stop letting him into his bed!

"No dogs at your house except Cocoa." Pedro recited the rule they'd all heard a hundred times. "I don't think your mom would ever make an exception to that, even for this little thing."

"True, unfortunately," Morgan said. If it were up to her, she'd have a half dozen of her own pups in addition to the Sterling dogs-in-training. As far as she was concerned, dogs were better than people. And definitely better than siblings.

Shelby rose from her chair, stretching and brushing tiny black and white hairs off her jeans. Dusty left a lot of fur for a little dog.

"Shelby, you're a mess!" Morgan blurted, seeing how fuzzed-up her sister had gotten. Morgan clamped her hand over her mouth, realizing her mistake, and braced for her older sister's reaction. Shelby used to love dogs as much as Morgan, but since she started high school last year, the oldest Sterling couldn't stand having dog hair—or slobber or anything dog-related—on her clothes.

Shelby gave a couple more brushes at the hair and shrugged. Normally the state of her clothes would be intolerable, but this was *Dusty's* hair. And nothing about Dusty was intolerable. Ever. "Oh well," she said lightly. "If that's the price I pay for the honor of having this little angel on my lap, then so be it!" She was being a bit over-the-top, she knew, but she was in a terrific mood. Last month's thwarted opportunity to go to the movies with a group of friends—including you-know-who—was getting a rain check tonight! Alice had just texted, and Shelby only had to float the idea past her mom . . .

Morgan's nose wrinkled in confusion. "Do you have a fever or something?"

Shelby flushed. "Of course not. It's just that he's . . . that I'm . . . oh, whatever. I just don't care."

"He's a charmer, huh?" Pedro asked, nodding. "I like him a lot myself. I've got to find a home for him, though. He's been here close to four weeks and it's time for him to start his new life." He felt a pang in his chest as the words lingered in the air, but he forged ahead. "I've been putting it off, but I'm committed to making some calls tonight. Have we gotten any response to your posts?"

Shelby's embarrassed expression morphed into one of anguish . . . and also guilt. She didn't want to tell him that she hadn't posted a single announcement about the center's adoptable dog. She hadn't meant to procrastinate this long and had typed up a cute description. But every time she went to post it she just couldn't. She shook her head, unable to explain.

"Well, we're off," Pedro said. "We will see you ladies tomorrow, when you can have him on your lap all day."

Shelby smiled at that. Yes, tomorrow was Saturday!

Like he did every evening, Dusty kept his ears up and his nose high as they walked the path to the trailer. Until he arrived at the ranch he'd had to use his nose to smell for one thing and one thing only: food. Now he was noticing ALL the smells. It had taken a while to adjust, but at this point his nose was free to sniff the world. There were so many smells, and he could discern them all! There was dirt and dog and trees and rubble and Morgan and Pedro and Forrest and Shelby and rabbit and squirrel and lots of deer poop. For a dog it was a cornucopia of delights!

When they were past the bus, Pedro set Dusty onto the ground and he ran to the door. He loved the cozy cavern where he and Pedro spent their evenings. "I know you've eaten, but I haven't!" Pedro announced as he opened the trailer door. He warmed up a can of soup and made several pieces of toast, while Dusty kept watch by the window. When he heard the clatter of dishes going into the sink, Dusty came and settled on the couch with Pedro and his bag of cookies. "These aren't for you," Pedro warned.

But Dusty already knew. He didn't get people food.

Tonight Pedro had a pad of paper and a little book. Instead of turning on the big light-up rectangle, he talked into the little one he carried in his pocket. Dusty couldn't understand the words, but he could tell that Pedro was mixed up inside. He smelled sad and determined. Dusty put his paws on Pedro's chest, licked his cheek, and then lay belly-up beside him, inviting him to do something more fun like rub his belly.

Pedro let out a long breath and gave Dusty a nice stomach scratching.

Shelby wasn't the only one who would miss this little guy . . . Pedro would, too.

10

Shelby tapped her foot impatiently and shot a look toward Morgan, who was still perusing books. Her mood had darkened since Dusty's departure, which, she'd noticed, happened almost every day.

"Haven't you read all of those books . . . like, five times each?" she asked pointedly.

Morgan ignored her, which soured Shelby's mood even more. "Can you step on it?" she huffed, picking at a blue-painted fingernail.

Morgan tossed a look over her shoulder. She had in fact read most of these books multiple times, but that didn't mean there wasn't value in reading them again. You couldn't absorb all the information on the first—or even second—read. Dogs and dog training were incredibly nuanced. That was one of the things she loved about them both.

"What's your hurry?" she tossed back. "Got a date or something?" To her surprise Shelby ducked her head as if to hide her expression. Morgan smiled to herself. Bingo!

"Of course not," Shelby sputtered. "I just, I mean . . . let's go!"

Morgan didn't press. She simply snatched *Dog Training Trials and Triumphs* and *Breeding Isn't Everything* off the shelf and breezily made her way to the door, where Shelby was waiting and jangling the keys in her hand. Shelby yanked the door closed behind them and locked up, rushing past her sister along the pathway to the Sterling house. Her heart was pounding fast. She didn't have much time to change before the movie, and being able to go at all might take some convincing. Georgia Sterling was no pushover.

"Mo-om!" she shouted as she raced through the door, bombarding her mother in the kitchen. "Alice invited me to the movies. There's a group of us going.

I've already started Monday's homework, and we'll be back by ten," she said breathlessly. She threw in every bit of information that might help her cause. She could *not* make this sound like a date. And it wasn't a date . . . she just *wished* it was a date. Kind of. Maybe.

She rocked back and forth on her toes while she waited for her mother's response. Georgia blinked several times and opened her mouth to reply just as Morgan strolled through the kitchen door with her nose in a book. Shoot! Shelby had wanted this conversation to be private.

"That sounds fun," Georgia said, pulling a can of beans out of the cupboard. "You should take your sisters."

"Take us where?" Morgan asked, glancing up from the first chapter of *Dog Training Trials and Triumphs*. Shelby turned away from both of them and closed her eyes to keep from rolling them . . . Eye rolling was her mother's pet peeve and strictly verboten and the kind of behavior that made her mom break into German. This was *not* what she had in mind!

It was clearly what her mother suddenly had in

mind, however, and Georgia was running with it. "Shelby's taking you to the movies," she told Morgan.

"Really?" Morgan's face lit up. She loved a good movie, and her books would be waiting when she got home.

The girls' mother was nodding and now held her phone in her hand. "I'll text Alice's mom to see if she has room in the car. Your father can pick all of you up."

Shelby bit her tongue. The last thing she wanted was to have to drag half her family to the movies . . . with Ryan! Still, she consoled herself, it was better than not being able to go at all. And there had been no mention of taking Forrest. She needed to quit while she was ahead.

"Okay, fine," she said, trying to sound cheerful enough to avoid an "attitude" discussion with her mother. "I'm going to change." She half smiled at Morgan and rushed upstairs to the bathroom, only to find the door closed.

"Juniper!" she called, knocking loudly. Her eight-year-old sister was capable of spending hours on end in the bathroom—and often did. But Shelby needed to pee and make sure she didn't look like she just rolled out of bed . . . or spent the afternoon with a dog on her lap! She made a quick decision. "Get out here or I won't take you to the movies!"

The door was open in a flash. "The movies?" Juniper asked, her eyes wide with excitement.

"Yes, the movies. With me and Morgan."

"Reeeooowww!"

"Oh, boys, I know. I'll miss you, too." Juniper turned toward Twig and Bud, who sat on the vanity. While Bud gazed at himself in the mirror, Twig licked the younger cat's neck. They were both wearing bonnets.

"There's room for everyone in Alice's car, but you all need to be out front in ten minutes," Georgia shouted up the stairs.

"Out. Now. Or you're not coming," Shelby growled.

Juniper snatched up the cats and flounced out of the bathroom, leaving it mercifully vacant.

With no time to shower, Shelby quickly washed her face and swept her hair into a loose half-back style.

In the bedroom she shared with Morgan, she slipped into her favorite sweater and dabbed essential oil on her wrists, wishing her mother would let her wear real perfume.

"Let's go!" she shouted as she took the stairs two at a time. Her sisters were already waiting at the door.

"You don't have to shout," Juniper replied with a slow blink and a toss of her braids.

Sighing and with both of her sisters in tow, Shelby raced out to the parking lot in front of the ranch.

The back seat of the car was crowded, and Shelby was relieved when, fifteen minutes later, they pulled up outside the theater.

"Have fun!" Alice's mom called as they piled out of the car. Ryan, Saul, and Beth were already there, waiting by the ticket line.

Shelby let Alice walk ahead to greet them, then turned to her sisters.

"After I get your tickets I want you guys to go sit by yourselves," she said.

Morgan couldn't resist the opportunity to tease her older sister. "Oh, so this *is* a . . ." Morgan stopped when she saw the look of anguish on Shelby's face. "I mean so long as popcorn is the first priority, we're good with that. Right, June?"

Juniper was staring through the window at the concession stand. "Only if there are also Milk Duds!"

Their mom didn't give them money for snacks, but it only took Shelby a split second to decide it would be worth it to spend her welcome center work allowance on snacks if it would mean getting her sisters off her back. They bought three tickets and headed inside to the snack line. After waiting ten minutes and forking out half of her savings—out of which all she got was one medium soda—Shelby finally wrenched herself free and joined her friends.

As Alice's careful planning would have it, Shelby's saved seat was right next to Ryan's. "Thanks," she mouthed to her friend as she stepped over Alice's long legs to the second seat in. The trailers had ended and the movie was starting, which was a-okay with Shelby because she was so nervous her tongue felt as dry as a dog biscuit. She couldn't even manage a simple hello to the adorable dark-haired boy sitting next to her!

Settled into her seat, she stared straight ahead at the screen. The movie was a comedy she'd been wanting to see, but she couldn't focus on the story. For one thing, she was sitting next to Ryan! For another, her heart was pounding so loudly in her ears she was one hundred percent certain half the theater could hear it. She fidgeted and tried to see what Ryan was doing without turning her head. As far as she could tell he was totally engrossed in the actors on the big screen.

Shelby tried to breathe and focus, and eventually found herself getting wrapped up in the story. She was really starting to root for the main character when she felt something touch her wrist. At first she started. But then she realized it was Ryan reaching for her hand! She opened her palm, and his fingers wrapped shyly around hers.

Shelby's face warmed and she smiled the widest smile of her life. His hand was warm and smooth and fit perfectly with hers. She sat back, happy and unbelieving. They. Were. Holding. Hands!

Shelby turned her head to see Ryan's expression in

the dark and noticed his eyes were glistening. He was tearing up at the sweet story on the screen! Shelby's heart melted a little, and she scooted closer and squeezed his hand, beaming in his direction and hoping he would look in her direction. Instead he jerked his hand away to cover his face. A second later he made a stifled, exploding sound. Then another. Shelby tried to lean closer to ask if he was okay, but her sleeve snagged the lid of the soda, jerking it out of the cup holder and upending the whole drink into Ryan's lap.

"Ugh!" Ryan jumped to his feet.

"Dude!" someone called from the back. Someone else shushed them.

Ryan swatted at his crotch while he continued to make stifled, exploding sounds. Sneezes! He sneezed louder and louder.

"Sit down or leave!" the guy behind them hissed.

Covering his nose with his elbow, Ryan made a beeline for the aisle, tripping and knocking Alice's popcorn everywhere along the way. Shelby shot Alice a look of utter desperation. She had no idea what to do!

"Go after him!" Alice whispered fiercely.

Shelby gulped. Um, okay . . .

When she got to the lobby, Shelby's eyes darted frantically to every corner, but Ryan was nowhere to be seen. She was wondering if he might be in the bathroom, when she spotted him on the sidewalk through the window. He held a wad of tissue under his nose with one hand and was using the other to blot the large wet spot on his pants. Shelby rushed outside in time to hear a couple of kids in line for another show laughing.

"Just couldn't make it, huh?" one of them laughed.

Shelby gaped. It looked *exactly* like he had peed his pants.

"It's soda!" Ryan shouted at them. Shelby willed the ground to swallow her up. She'd never seen Ryan so upset. She'd never even heard him raise his voice!

As she approached she could see that his dark eyes were puffy and red. Was he so embarrassed he was crying? She had to admit she would have been mortified, too. The wet splotch was covered in bits of white shreds that looked just like toilet paper.

He looked at her, squinting, and started sneezing all over again. Shelby's stomach churned. She felt sick. This was her fault, and he must hate her!

"Stay back," he said. "I can't take anymore . . ." Their eyes met for a moment, and his voice softened. "Please," he said. "Just go."

Shelby felt her heart leap into her throat. She wanted to apologize. She wanted to help. But he didn't want her around. There was only one thing to do. Her eyes welling with tears, she turned and walked hurriedly away.

11

Martin Sterling stuck his head into the canine pavilion. He was looking for Pedro but spotted Forrest and Morgan instead. "Have you two seen Pedro?" he called to them.

The pair looked up from where they were busily scrubbing kennels and filling bowls for the entourage of canines. They were up early this Saturday. They had been back to school for almost two months, and as their parents constantly reminded them, school was their real job, and always came first. So when the weekend rolled around, they both got up early to maximize their dog time.

"Sorry, Dad," Forrest called. Morgan looked up

and shook her head. She hadn't seen him, either.

Martin checked his watch. He was a little early, but Pedro was usually early, too. He took the extra moment to walk down the center row of dog enclosures, greeting each wagging trainee along the way. There were about half a dozen Labs and border collies and golden retrievers, all rested and ready for work—which, in their doggy brains, was pure fun. Martin understood. He always found a way to make his job fun, too.

"Martin!" Pedro entered the pavilion a moment later with his hand out and wearing a smile. The two men shook hands, patted shoulders, and fell into conversation.

Forrest strained to hear what the adults were talking about. Two or three words coming out of his dad's mouth made him wish he had ears like the Chihuahua who had taken up residence on Shelby's lap. He stepped closer.

"Did you just say there are two dump trucks on their way to the ranch?" Forrest interrupted. Then he looked a little sheepish. His mom would give him a look or a lecture for interrupting, and he knew it was rude. But his dad understood his exuberance and clapped his hands together instead.

"You heard right," he confirmed. "We're getting a double load of construction debris for the rubble pile."

Morgan had been listening, too. And watching. What she saw made her smile. Her dad, her brother, and Pedro all looked like little kids who'd been given permission to take the hose into the sand box. They were about to have some good messy fun, and the ranch was about to get an upgrade.

The rubble pile was where the dogs practiced the incredible agility necessary to stay safe when searching after disasters like earthquakes, hurricanes, landslides, and explosions that left destruction in their wakes. It was already quite large, but to keep the dogs on their toes, literally, the training area needed constant refreshing and expanding.

"I'll go wait for the trucks so I can guide them in," Pedro said. "Just have to run back to my place first."

Martin nodded. "Great. I'll go make sure the site's ready."

"And I'm going to come with you?" Forrest asked his dad with a "please, please, please" grin and held up two sets of crossed fingers.

His dad cracked up. "All right. If you're done here." Martin shot a glance at Morgan and raised his eyebrows. It looked like the kids had completed the morning dog chores, but he didn't want Forrest running off and leaving Morgan to finish the work.

Forrest gazed at Morgan with the same hopeful, pleading look he'd given their dad.

Morgan relented with an amused roll of her dark eyes. They were almost done, and she really didn't mind. "Fine. Go play with trucks." She waved a hand at them.

Forrest was out the door first, shouting over his shoulder, "Don't forget the skid loader! We're gonna use that, too, right, Dad?"

The skid loader was already parked by the heap of debris, ready to prep for and adjust the new shipment of rubble. It took a lot of effort and skill to create a pile that replicated destroyed buildings.

"Can I drive it?" Forrest asked, rushing up to the miniature excavator.

"Nope." Martin shook his head. Forrest had been bugging him to drive the skid loader since he was about four years old. "But you can ride with me if you want," he offered.

Forrest could have predicted that answer and was already climbing up into the cab so he could perch behind his dad while they shifted the pile with the giant metal bucket attachment on the front. Looking over his father's shoulder, Forrest studied his every move. When his dad finally said yes to letting him drive, he'd be ready.

The two Sterlings lifted some of the larger beams and moved them to the side. Martin had flags over the areas where he'd installed "hides"—larger covered places for training assistants to conceal themselves and wait for dogs-in-training to locate them. They were going for another run to push the pile higher and make room for the dump when Forrest spotted Pedro hurrying toward them. He was tugging on his goatee . . . something he only did when he was thinking, or worried.

Forrest tapped his dad's shoulder and pointed. Martin cut the engine.

"Have you seen Dusty?" Pedro asked, out of breath. "He got out of the trailer. I was just going to take him to Shelby, but I can't find him."

Martin and Forrest both shook their heads. "No lap rat here," Forrest said. "Maybe Shelby went and got him?" It sounded possible. Shelby was hardly ever away from Dusty lately and had, like, zero patience.

"Maybe," Pedro said, but he didn't think it sounded like something Shelby would do. She loved the little pup, but . . . he turned to check in with Shelby just as she appeared on the path, empty-handed. She lifted one arm up in a wave, and Forrest felt his heart sink a little.

"Hey, Pedro! I came to take Dusty off your hands!" Shelby called, spotting the guys by the rubble pile. She scanned the area, looking for her favorite black-and-white companion. Then she looked at Pedro, who was stroking his whiskers. "Where is he?" she asked as worry crept into her voice.

"I was just coming to ask you if you knew," Pedro told her. "The little Houdini must have gotten out of the trailer."

Shelby bit her bottom lip. She tried not to panic. She'd been acting like she was doing Pedro a favor by watching Dusty. What nobody seemed to understand was that she *needed* the little dog's company. Ever since the awful movie calamity, she'd been feeling awful about *everything* and *everyone* with a single exception: Dusty. She couldn't explain why, but the micro mutt made her feel . . . better. "So, he's *missing*?" Her voice broke.

"I'm not sure," Pedro answered slowly. "I guess, yes. He's kind of . . . missing. But he can't have gone far."

"Not on those legs," Forrest joked. Nobody laughed.

"Missing" was not a word Shelby wanted to hear. She gasped for air and started to shake her hands like there was something sticky and gross on them that she wanted to get off.

Martin climbed out of the loader. "Easy, Shel. Everything's okay." He put a hand around his oldest daughter's shoulders. He knew her tendency to make mountains out of molehills and wanted to talk her down before she was too far gone. "Panicking isn't going to help," he said reasonably. "He's never run away before and he survived for a long time on his own. He's probably at the pavilion, or dumpster-diving for food in the refuse area."

Shelby stopped shaking. She leaned into her dad, still looking doubtful. Martin was about to start delegating search areas when they heard the rumble of the trucks that had found their way to the rubble pile without a guide.

"Hold that thought," Martin told Shelby. The search was going to have to be postponed until the delivery was made—he couldn't keep the drivers waiting. Shelby let out a shuddering breath and leaned on the skid loader, biting a blue-painted fingernail.

"Right in here. Close as you can get!" Martin yelled to the first driver, who was already maneuvering the dump truck toward the pile. Forrest grabbed the nearby hose and started spraying the area where the big load of rebar, wood, concrete, bricks, and steel beams would be deposited. He'd helped with this before and knew that before and during the dump it was important to spray the area to keep the dust down.

Forlorn, Shelby watched for a minute, and then headed back to the welcome center to see if Dusty was waiting for her there.

The first load slid out of the tilted truck bed with a resounding racket and a huge cloud of dust (in spite of the spray). Forrest kept dousing everything with the hose, getting as close as his dad would let him. After lowering its bed, the first truck made way for the second. Martin asked the second driver to drop his haul in two loads so it would be easier to spread around and not bury the covert hiding areas he'd installed. It was important to have multiple hides at the top, middle, and bottom layers of the pile. It was also important to keep the pile shifting. Dog training was all about continuous learning and preparing for the unknown.

Before they knew it an hour had passed. Martin checked his phone. He had thirteen texts from Shelby asking if they'd seen Dusty. He suspected her nails were down to the nubs.

Sorry. Haven't seen him. I'll send Pedro back to check his trailer.

Forrest stopped spraying and came to stand next to his dad. The trucks rumbled away and the area grew quiet. Martin was torn. Should he leave off work and go look for the scrap of dog, or keep going and get the pile ready for the teams anxious to train on it and hope that Dusty showed up with a belly full of something on his own? He ran his hand through the little hair he had left. The Chihuahua wasn't an official Sterling dog, but he had a soft spot for the little mutt and his big attitude. At the moment he could picture his silly winglike ears and hear his decisive yaps—Dusty had a big bark for a small dog. He was pretty sure that everyone at the ranch was smitten with Dusty.

"Yip!"

Martin jerked his chin up. He looked at Forrest. Forrest looked at Pedro. They heard it, too.

"Yip! Yip!" The muffled sound came again. The bark was unmistakable. It was definitely Dusty. And it was definitely coming from inside the football-field-sized pile of debris!

12

Pedro, Forrest, and Martin froze. None of them moved or even breathed as they waited to hear another bark from deep in the massive pile. It was so quiet they could have heard a single leaf fall from the nearby scrub oak, but that wasn't what they were waiting to hear . . .

"Yip!" The bark finally came. It was insistent but muffled—buried deep in the heap of treacherous construction debris.

Suddenly Shelby appeared on the path. She'd seen the trucks leave and couldn't just sit in the welcome center while Dusty was missing! She rushed up to her dad, brother, and Pedro. They were all standing there like rusted tin men—not moving. "What's going on?" she asked, confused. If they hadn't *found* Dusty, why weren't they searching?

A muffled "Yip!" was her answer.

"Wait! That's him! He's in there!" Shelby gasped. She stared wide-eyed at the horrifying pile. She did not want to imagine Dusty, who was no bigger than a cantaloupe, trapped inside a mountain of dangerous junk. He could so easily be smashed or skewered! They had to get him out. Now!

Forrest lurched toward the pile, ready to start pulling it apart with his bare hands, but Martin held him back.

"Hold on. We can't go charging in there. The pile is unstable. One wrong step and we might cause a collapse."

Pedro nodded. He was having trouble holding himself back, too. Especially when Dusty yipped again. But he knew Martin was right. He ran his hand over his bearded chin, feeling awful. He was the reason Dusty was in this mess. He felt determination rise—determination to get the little pup out safely. He just had no idea *how*.

"We have to do something!" Shelby wailed. She was fighting tears and looking up at the mass towering over their heads. The mountain of garbage took on a whole new meaning with Dusty trapped inside it. The jagged edges of broken concrete, the broken beams, the twisted pipes . . . It was a terrible snare filled with deadly pitfalls!

Pedro held up a hand, and the group went silent again. They listened carefully. Dusty's bark had moved.

"Dusty!" Pedro called to the dog. "We hear you, amigo. Come to us." To the others he said, "Let's give him a chance to get out on his own. It might be the safest way. If anyone can move around in there, he can."

"But—" Shelby started to protest. What if he was hurt? What if he couldn't move? She tried to keep the awful thoughts at bay.

Martin put an arm around his daughter's shoulders. "He's small and light enough that he might not disturb the pile. He just has to find a way out."

"And rats are great at maneuvering in garbage . . ." Forrest said. He meant it to be comforting, but the uncharacteristically stern look his dad shot him shut him up. He started walking the perimeter of the unstable hill, listening intently.

Dusty kept barking.

"Good dog," Pedro murmured when it was clear the sound was traveling. "He's letting us know he's alive . . . and moving."

"Wait, does it sound different?" Shelby asked, cocking her head to one side. "Is he getting closer?"

"We can't be certain. Sounds and smells bounce around in debris piles, making them hard to interpret." Pedro didn't want to add that it takes months, sometimes years, to train SAR dogs to successfully navigate disaster piles. They spent a long time working on agility before they were even allowed to approach loose debris.

For several seconds there was no new sound. Then, "Yip!"

The next bark sounded different. They couldn't say exactly where it was coming from, but it was definitely in a new place. Dusty could move around in there . . . at least a little.

"Yip!"

Shelby stepped toward the edge of the pile. The bark seemed to be coming from a tiny gap in the recent dump. Her eyes were bright with tears as she stared at the dark crack the sound seemed to be coming out of. "He's so close, we have to help! We need to dig for him!"

"We can't," her dad insisted, though it was taking all his resolve not to start dismantling the pile himself. "It's not settled. It could all come down and—"

"Flat rat," Forrest said quietly. Not quietly enough.

Shelby tried to take a deep breath. It caught halfway. She gulped and followed the sound of the bark as it curved along the edge of the pile. It got higher, then dropped away. "Come on, Dusty!" she called out in encouragement. "We're right here!"

"There!" Forrest pointed to a spot near the top of the scrap heap. Twenty feet up there was tiny movement. The tip of Dusty's scarred ear appeared through a slot between a slab of concrete and a thick wooden beam. The opening was too small for even the teensy Chihuahua to come through.

"Dusty!" Shelby clutched her hands together near her throat and called out at the same moment that the pile moved. The heavy trash shifted like quicksand and sent up a rumble and a cloud of dust. "No!" Shelby shouted.

Martin turned ghostly pale. Pedro winced. He started to call out a stay command—which is what he would do if he were working with a trained dog to keep him safe. If only Dusty were trained, he might be able to help him navigate!

"Why isn't he barking?" Shelby asked when the pile had settled. Then, before anyone could answer, Dusty wriggled out of the small opening. He scrambled up out of the pile and walked along a narrow board with the agility of a gymnast.

It took all of Shelby's willpower not to scale the treacherous hill and grab him in a hug.

"Dusty!" Forrest crowed.

The tiny dog stopped on the board he was

navigating. It teetered. Shelby drew in a breath. Dusty froze. He held his position until the board settled, then, carefully placing his paws as if he was in the middle of a choreographed dance, made it to the other end. With all eyes glued on him, Dusty calculated each step. He ducked under rebar, hopped onto a broken culvert, and made it to solid ground, where a very happy, very relieved crew of people awaited him.

Shelby reached the dog first and scooped him up close to her face. He was dirty and dusty but happy to lick the cheek of the girl he adored. He'd had a grand adventure!

"Careful," Pedro cautioned. He wanted to check the dog for injuries. It wasn't clear how the little guy had gotten out of the depths of the pile, and he could be hurt. The truck could have dumped on top of him! Shelby placed the dog on the ground, and Pedro gently felt his back and head and legs while Dusty stood straighter than a show dog. He was obviously proud. As soon as Pedro pronounced him unscathed, Shelby had him back in her arms.

"You are some dog," Pedro said, shaking his head.

Even Forrest was deeply impressed. "He walked that pile like he's been doing it all his life!"

"I guess sometimes it helps to be small," Martin said with raised eyebrows.

Everyone agreed. In the face of a dangerous mountain of trash, Dusty's tiny size was a huge asset.

13

Morgan helped her dad put the last leaf into the Sterling dining room table, and they pushed the ends together, expanding it to its maximum capacity. *Everyone* was coming for dinner, including Morgan's grandma; her dog, Cocoa; the center's lead trainer and Morgan's hero, Roxanne; Pedro; and Dusty. They would be twelve including the dogs and fourteen if you counted cats, which Juniper would probably insist upon.

"Here." Morgan counted out ten placemats from a drawer in the sideboard and handed them to her little sister. It was the kids' job to set the table. Juniper doled the red woven mats out onto the dark wood like playing cards and then straightened them. Morgan followed her dad to the kitchen. She took a deep breath, breathing in cheesy, tomatoey goodness. Her mom's lasagna was a family favorite. Make that a *ranch* favorite. Pedro was already in the kitchen, hovering near the stove and ready for the first piece. Morgan had noticed that even when he wasn't invited, Pedro always managed to show up on lasagna night. She was pretty sure he could smell it baking from his trailer!

"What is your secret?" Pedro asked. "You make the best lasagna I've *ever* tasted!"

Georgia gave Pedro a sly smile. "Let's just say that Italians brought their *food* to Eritrea, and the Eritreans brought their *taste* to Italian food!"

Georgia winked at Morgan, and Morgan winked back. Her mom's Eritrean lasagna was way better than the sloppy stuff she'd had in Italian restaurants. She knew the secret ingredient was spicy berbere, but she wouldn't give it away. Her mom liked being able to lure people to her table.

"Hi! Hope I'm not late!" Roxanne arrived in the

kitchen, followed by Martin and Frances, who had been chatting in the living room. "Can I do anything?" Roxanne asked.

"I think we're all ready. Your timing is perfect," Georgia said. She carried the heavy dish of lasagna to the table, which Forrest and Juniper had just finished setting. Frances brought in a big salad, and Martin added a long loaf of bread spread with garlic butter and sprinkled with oregano.

Forrest couldn't wait to dig in after his long day. He was starving! But one seat was still empty: Shelby's.

"Morgan, can you go get your sister?" Georgia asked. She put her napkin on her lap and exhaled slowly. Shelby had not been herself lately—she'd been quiet, absent. When she joined them at the table, Georgia peered at her oldest while she served herself half the amount of lasagna she usually did.

"Honey?" Martin interrupted his wife's thoughts. He was holding the giant bowl of salad midair. "Salad?"

Georgia forced a smile and tried to tune in to the

conversation and tune out her concerns about Shelby. Everyone was talking about Dusty. The little dog had caused a big stir.

"I think he knows we're talking about him!" Juniper pointed at the tiny dog, who had taken over Cocoa's enormous bed. Curled in the center, he looked even smaller than usual.

"Of course he does," Pedro laughed. "Look at his ears!"

Dusty's triangle ears stood up straight, like over-sized tortilla chips, catching every sound. His nose was tucked under his paws, and Pedro could have sworn he was hiding a smile. "You should have seen him, Roxanne. Forrest isn't kidding. He was a natural on that pile. He could pass your agility training in a heartbeat! He'd put your dogs to shame!"

Everyone around the table laughed . . . everyone but Shelby.

Roxanne dabbed her eyes with her napkin. "That good, eh?"

"He's wonderful company," Pedro said. "But he could be more than a pet. Much more. Now that he's feeling better he is getting feisty. I think he needs work to keep himself out of trouble."

Shelby nodded without smiling. It was true. "He has a great nose, and those ears don't miss a thing. He's fast. He's smart. Independent but not too headstrong." She started listing his attributes, not including the fact that ever since the fiasco at the movies—where she'd made Ryan run from her—Dusty was the only thing that made her feel remotely good. It was like she was living inside a dark cloud and the little dog was the only ray of light.

Georgia stopped chewing when she realized what Shelby was saying, and what it would mean for her. She was encouraging the team to consider Dusty for SAR training. If they decided to train him, the pup would no longer be able to spend his days on her lap. He'd go from being a pet to being a work dog practically overnight. It would be a huge sacrifice for the high schooler.

"Are you saying you think Dusty has SAR potential?" Georgia asked. She looked from Shelby to Pedro while Roxanne choked back a laugh. Martin sat back in his chair and drummed his fingers lightly on the table.

"He's a wonderful dog," Roxanne said. "And smart, for sure. But he's just so . . ."

"Tiny," Forrest finished for her. "*Seriously* tiny. I weighed him this morning, and he still only weighs nine pounds."

"That's nine pounds of determination and smarts," Shelby insisted, a bit of spark returning. "He can do it! He can do anything. You saw him today!"

"I am sure Dusty can do a lot of things, but there are many factors to consider. There's no way he can cover as much territory as a larger dog, and does a dog his size have the reserves or the stamina to put in a full shift?" Roxanne wondered out loud.

Forrest took a big bite of bread. There was a long silence while everyone chewed.

"I can't argue those points," Pedro finally said. "But I think the little guy deserves a shot. We're not too heavy on dogs-in-training right now, and they recently certified a twelve-pound dog in Japan."

Roxanne looked at Pedro. The two were partners,

but she made the calls on the dogs and he was in charge of humans. It was the first time he was advising her on canines.

"Twelve pounds is almost as big as a Dusty and a half," she said. She just wasn't convinced, and the last thing she wanted was to put the little dog in danger.

"He's also curious, and he's never had issues with other dogs," Shelby added. Small-dog attitude could cause fear aggression, which was a deal breaker. "And he doesn't show aggression around food, either." They all knew that was rare in a dog who'd spent months on the edge of starvation.

Georgia watched the conversation without comment. Her dark eyes took in everything. Though she was in charge of the day-to-day operations at Sterling, this was not her decision. When it came to selecting dogs to train, it was up to Roxanne. If she wanted a second opinion, she asked Pedro. Georgia and Martin and Frances were generally included in the conversation, but they were not the decision makers. What was unusual about this situation was that Pedro and

Roxanne disagreed. That had never happened before.

The silence around the table grew.

"Um, if you're thinking about training a micro dog with giant rabbit ears, why aren't we talking about training a brilliant kitten like Bud?" Juniper piped up. She pointed to the small, mostly gray kitten who had strolled into the dining room and settled down next to Cocoa by the radiator. "He has great agility and great eyesight. He's even smarter than Twig, and we all know Twig is a genius and a natural search and rescue cat. I mean, he saved an entire litter of kittens who'd lost their mother!" The littlest Sterling pursed her lips and lifted her chin defiantly, looking at the adults sitting around the table in turn.

Roxanne and Pedro had to look at their laps to keep from laughing. The eight-year-old was dead serious.

"If anyone can train a cat, it's you, June Bug." Her dad gave her the only vote of confidence. It was true. Juniper's tenacity was astronomical. "But we're talking about Dusty."

"Are you sure you're not biased, Pedro? Because Dusty came from your niece? Or maybe because you want to keep him around?" Roxanne asked, bringing the conversation back to Dusty. Like her dogs-in-training, Roxanne never lost the thread—she was tracking information that would lead to the right decision, the way her dogs stayed on a trail until they found their objective. She looked at Pedro with sharp green eyes that were open and inquisitive. She did not mince words, or shy away from tough questions. She studied her partner's body language, searching for unspoken clues.

Pedro was quiet for a good minute. The conversation had turned extremely serious. "I can't deny it. I like this dog. I'm attached," he answered honestly.

Shelby nodded silently. She was attached, too.

"But, that aside, his agility today was remarkable, and I think he deserves to be evaluated. He's healthy enough for us to do an assessment, and we can do that without straining our program or ourselves." Pedro's dark eyes were questioning, not demanding. He didn't want to push.

Roxanne looked to Frances, who had been uncharacteristically quiet. The matriarch usually had a story to relate, pulled from her years of experience. Nobody refuted her keen intuition when it came to assessing dogs or risks. But today Frances returned Roxanne's gaze silently, and the younger woman could tell by the elder's expression that she'd decided to keep quiet. She was leaving it up to her.

"I think he deserves to be evaluated," Morgan said softly. At ten, Morgan was by far the quietest of the Sterling kids, the resident animal whisperer, and the savviest about training. She could easily be the next Roxanne, or even the next Frances Sterling.

Every head at the table turned to look at Morgan. This was the first time she'd spoken since they sat down, and her comment carried weight. It didn't wash away all of Roxanne's reservations, but it did tip the scales.

"All right," Roxanne agreed. "We'll take him through the basics tomorrow, and let the results speak for themselves."

Shelby and Pedro heaved sighs of relief. Morgan saw them catch each other's eyes . . . the Dusty fan club. She smiled to herself. Being the quiet one could come in handy; when she chose to speak up, her voice came through loud and clear.

14

Shelby sat behind the welcome center desk, biting her cuticles. It had been a long week, and it was only Tuesday. She glanced down at her cold, empty lap. She missed Dusty any time he wasn't with her, and today was particularly hard. Today Dusty was being assessed to see if he was search and rescue material.

Shelby sighed. She'd lobbied for the Chihuahua to be given a shot at training. She *wanted* this for him. But sometimes you wanted things that hurt, too. She knew she should be happy, and she was, deep down. But she was sad, too. Sad that he was somewhere else, sad that she couldn't see him being assessed, and saddest of all about what she knew in her heart: Dusty was going to leave the ranch to become a search and rescue dog.

She had tried to convince one of her siblings to cover her desk duties so she could watch Dusty's assessment. She asked her brother first, and Forrest straight up turned her down. Morgan, whom she could usually talk into anything, was next. Morgan reluctantly told her no, too. Apparently Roxanne had promised that she could help with the assessment. Shelby had been a little heartbroken but didn't give Morgan a hard time. She knew her younger sister would do anything to be involved in training. And unfortunately, there was no point in asking Juniper for help. She was too young to work the desk.

Inspecting her thumbnail for any remaining bits of polish she could scrape off, Shelby tried not to fidget. She was so anxious that when her phone pinged she jumped. It was a message from Alice.

How's your boyfriend?

The word "boyfriend" made Shelby's face get hot even though Alice wasn't talking about Ryan. She knew better than that. Ryan talk had been off-limits since the movie incident. Shelby had been avoiding him at school, too, which meant she'd also been avoiding most of her friends. The whole thing was making her miserable, which was why Alice knew better than to bring it up.

She wasn't asking about Ryan . . . she was asking about Dusty. The tiny therapy dog she'd been spending as much time with as possible since "the incident."

No idea—they took him for assessment. Waiting to hear. Chewing my fingers off.

She added an emoji of painted nails and a grimacing face. Alice sent one back of crossed fingers.

Shelby looked at her empty lap again. She felt just as empty on the inside. She knew if Dusty passed assessment he wouldn't need constant care and holding—he'd be working most of the time. But, she argued with herself, having him accepted for training was the best way to keep him on the ranch for the longest time. Not to mention was what was best for him.

On the training grounds, the rest of the Sterling siblings were as tense as their oldest sister. Morgan and Forrest waited on the field. Juniper watched from the observation trailer with Pedro and Frances, holding not just Twig, but Twig and Bud! It was quite an armful and quite a crowd; Dusty had worked his way into each of their hearts as deftly as he'd worked his way out of the disaster pile!

Roxanne had already completed the first task. She'd walked with Dusty on-leash through the canine pavilion holding a toy—a squeaky bear as big as Dusty—that the Chihuahua was obsessed with. They'd walked rapidly, Roxanne checking continuously to see where Dusty's attention lay. Even as they passed by a dozen dogs, Dusty kept his eyes on the bear. That was good. He had focus.

Outside on the expansive training field, she held Dusty's toy out again. He dropped into a play bow, wagging. Then he grabbed the bear by the ear. Sure, he was so light Roxanne could pull him around the dusty field, but he didn't show any signs of letting go. With the little dog still clamped on to the toy, Roxanne raised a hand, signaling Morgan and Forrest.

Morgan went first. She banged two pans together, making a huge racket. Dusty looked to see what had made the sound but kept his jaws locked on the bear. That was also good.

Forrest was next. He stepped closer, holding his hands behind his back. All at once his right arm swung around. He popped an umbrella open, flung it on the ground, and stepped back. The sudden movement would alarm many dogs, making them cower or attack the startling object. Dusty gave a tiny hop sideways, a little side eye, and kept tugging.

Roxanne grinned. "You're a tough one, aren't you?" she said. She wouldn't have expected a street dog to be so unflappable.

Inside the trailer, Pedro cheered. "That's my guy!" he crowed. Though they'd just begun, Dusty was batting a thousand. In the distance Pedro could see Dusty's next challenge waiting patiently. Eloise, one of their training assistants, had brought her rottweiler, Harris, to lend a paw. Harris was all black except for the tan mask that covered most of his lower face. He also had two tan spots above his eyes, which made him look as though he was always asking a question. He was a huge love and also an unneutered male. If Dusty was going to have a fearful or aggressive reaction to another canine, it would be toward an intimidating dog like Harris.

Roxanne released the squeaky bear, and Dusty gave it a victory shake. Then he trotted around with it, making sure everyone saw his big win. He had to hold his head extra high to keep from tripping on the toy, which made everyone laugh. Roxanne took a few steps away and sat down on a bench at the edge of the training grounds. She wanted Dusty to be on his own for the next test.

Eloise and Harris approached slowly, just as Dusty was settling down to chew on his bear. When he saw the big dog coming closer, he stood and puffed out his chest. His tail started to wag.

"Good dog," Roxanne murmured to herself.

Dusty stood at attention, his ears like tiny sails,

while Harris approached. The big rotty gave him a thorough sniffing.

Inside the trailer, Frances chuckled. "I don't think your dog has any idea he's small," she said to Pedro.

Dusty wasn't "his" dog, but Pedro didn't correct her. "Harris could eat him in one bite, for seguro," he agreed proudly.

While the dogs sniffed and made friends, Roxanne signaled to Morgan again. The last assessment for the day was a search test. With Dusty distracted, Morgan snuck off with the beloved bear. Moving slowly, she walked to a set of seven barrels cut in half and lying side by side. Lifting one end, she stashed the bear in the third barrel before walking back to where she'd been watching from the shade structure.

The two dogs finally got their fill of smells and began to wander a little. Dusty went back to where he'd left his bear and noticed right away that he was gone. He sniffed the spot where the bear had been and raised his head to look around. Where was Bear? He sniffed again. Bear smelled like so many things he loved: Pedro's trailer, Cheetos, cotton stuffing, his pillow . . . Thinking about it made him want Bear more and more. He wanted to chew him and shake him and sleep on him! He sniffed the dusty ground. He lifted his nose and sniffed the air. There! Bear was over there!

Dusty ran to the barrels, barely bothering to sniff them. Through a tiny hole his nose pinpointed the scent. Bear was there! "Yip!" he barked at the third barrel. "Yip! Yip! Yip!"

Forrest cheered. Morgan clapped her hands together, and even from outside the trailer they could hear the observers celebrating Dusty's success, too.

Roxanne had to admit that Dusty's assessment had gone as well as any she'd seen. She lifted the barrel and let the Chihuahua get his reward. He pulled Bear out and trotted proudly around the field, showing him off to anyone and everyone.

"Well?" Morgan asked, running up to the trainer.

Roxanne knew that the pup had done well. But despite his impressive performance, there were still many things to consider.

Roxanne turned to Morgan. "So far, so good," she

said. "But there is a lot more to be seen."

Morgan felt a small wave of disappointment, but quickly pushed it aside. He'd done great so far, and she believed the tiny pup was destined to do amazing things.

15

"Mrowr." A spooky-sounding meow echoed down the stairs ahead of Juniper, who leaped into the hallway after it. The third grader was dressed in a tabby-striped pajama onesie with a tail and ears to match. Morgan had helped her draw whiskers on her cheeks, and she'd blackened a tiny triangle on the end of Juniper's nose to complete the feline effect.

"Here, kitty, kitty," Morgan called from the living room. Juniper slunk in, acting aloof—just like a cat—but secretly excited to show off her Halloween costume. She prowled back and forth in front of her parents.

"Oh!" Georgia clapped her hands together. "Baby,

you look fantastic!" Martin's booming laugh let everyone know he approved of the outfit as well. "It's purrrrfect," he said, chuckling.

"What do you think, Twig? Bud? We're practically twins!" Juniper sidled up to the cats sleeping beside Shelby on the couch. She pet them both with a mittened paw. While Bud purred, Twig opened his eyes, gave a disapproving glare to let Juniper know he did not like being woken up, and rested his head back on the cushion.

"I know I look good!" Juniper said, as if the cranky tabby had paid her a compliment. She pretended to lick her paw and ran it over the back of her headband ear.

"Where's your costume, Morgan?" Georgia asked.

"Oh, be right back!" Morgan had been so busy helping Juniper she'd almost forgotten. She raced back up the stairs, grateful her costume did not involve makeup.

Georgia glanced at Shelby sitting across the room in street clothes. She had a slightly haunted look about her, slumped on the couch. Her mom knew it had nothing to do with the holiday, however, and thought it might have everything to do with the boy she liked and had been avoiding.

"You sure you don't want to dress up and hang out with your friends tonight?" Georgia asked.

Shelby shook her head. "Nope. But I told Juniper I'd take her trick-or-treating." It had been a good excuse to give Alice and the others, and Shelby'd made sure to make it sound to her friends like it hadn't been her choice.

"Yes! Candy!" Juniper pumped her fist and practiced a cat leap. Just the thought of all the sugar headed her way had her amped up. "Let's go! Let's go!"

"Hold on, tuna breath." Shelby got up at the same time there was a knock at the back door. She opened it to find Pedro and Dusty on the porch. This was the other reason she'd agreed to take Juniper out . . . Pedro said she could take Dusty along. The crowds and costumes and strange noises would be good for him since rescue dogs needed to be prepared to deal with all kinds of new and strange situations.

"Thanks for bringing him over," Shelby said.

"No problemo." Pedro nodded, handing Dusty over. "I wanted to get him a costume but I didn't have time. I think he'd make a great Yoda."

"Or maybe a Gremlin!" Forrest hurtled into the hall dressed in a red jumpsuit and sandals like a tethered character from *Us*.

Shelby shuddered and held Dusty closer. "Creepy, bro."

Forrest reached over to give Dusty a pat. "You really should have dressed up like a kangaroo and kept that lap rat in your pouch like a joey!" Forrest laughed. Dusty's ears flattened.

Shelby narrowed her eyes. She opened her mouth to tell Forrest what she thought of his jokes but closed it again when she saw her parents standing together in the doorway looking at her with "concerned" faces.

Georgia stepped closer and scratched Dusty behind his ears while Shelby tucked him inside her jacket. She loved having the little dog close and immediately felt her breath deepening as she zipped him in.

"He really is a comfort to you, isn't he?" Georgia asked.

All Shelby could do was nod.

"So, are we ready?" Martin took the car keys off the hook in the hall. He was shuttling the whole crew to the best trick-or-treating spot in town. Looking around, he realized that they were one kid shy.

"Morgan!" he called. "Or should I say Serena?" He laughed as Morgan descended the steps dressed in a Serena Williams black tennis tutu and carrying a racket.

"Grand slam, my dear!" Georgia approved of her middle girl's costume. "Stay safe," she called as they traipsed out to the car. "And bring me some Skittles!"

During the ride, Morgan quietly offered Shelby a lace mask in the shape of a butterfly. "If you want," she told her.

Shelby accepted the offering and let Morgan help her tie it on. She knew her sister was worried about her. Her whole family was. They knew better than to fuss at her, which would be super irritating, but each of them in their own way had let her know they were concerned. They missed the old, happy Shelby, even if she could be a little snarky and a lot bossy.

With Dusty in her arms and her face mostly covered, Shelby felt almost okay as she climbed out of the car. At least she wouldn't have to worry about being recognized.

The sidewalks in Trestle Glen, which was one of those neighborhoods that went all out with the decorations and attracted a bazillion costumed kids and cost the neighbors a fortune in candy, were already crowded. Dusty craned his neck to take it all in. His round eyes were open wide, his ears twitched, and his teeny nostrils flared. He smelled greasy makeup, hair spray, caramel corn, chocolate, plastic, and fruity candy. He also smelled excitement wafting off the swarms of crazy creatures. There were box-headed robots, vampires with dripping fangs, rag dolls, superheroes, and monsters . . . and they all smelled like *kid*. It made him so happy he couldn't keep his tail still.

"Take it easy," Shelby chuckled. She didn't want Dusty to jump out of her jacket and go exploring on his own. It was hard enough to keep an eye on Juniper, who was racing from house to house in order to meet her goal of filling her pillowcase to the brim. Shelby peered over the crowd and spotted Juniper's ears, then stepped back to wait. She was having so much fun watching Dusty greet each kid that passed that she forgot to watch out for the friends she wanted to avoid until—

"Shelby!" Alice shouted her best friend's name. Shelby tried to duck her head, but it was too late. Alice launched herself through the crowd and practically tackled her in a hug. "I can't believe I found you! Oh!" Alice leaped back when she felt something wriggling between them. Dusty! "Oops! Sorry! I almost squished your boyfriend," Alice said loudly.

Too loudly. Shelby's jaw dropped open and then clamped tightly shut when she saw Ryan with the rest of their crew right behind Alice. She hoped he hadn't heard Alice. Ryan had on a cloak, Gryffindor tie, and Harry Potter glasses. He looked extra cute and his smile was extra wide, which wasn't helping. He stepped around Alice and took off his glasses . . . as if

Shelby wouldn't recognize him with them on. Shelby stepped back. The tree behind her and the surging crowd kept her from receding. Why was Ryan coming so close? She thought he hated her. Morgan's butterfly mask might have worked to conceal her identity at a distance, but he was standing right there! She wondered if he was finally going to tell her off for being such a klutz at the movies.

"Hi," Ryan said. Shelby was speechless. She wanted him to use his wand to make her disappear!

Dusty stretched his neck out toward Ryan as Shelby whirled. She stepped around the tree and tried to find a path through the crowd.

"Shelby, wait."

She felt a hand on her arm.

"I just want to talk to you." Ryan didn't sound mad. He sounded like he was asking for a favor.

Shelby stopped. She pulled off her mask. Slowly she turned around.

"Are you mad at me or something?" Ryan asked.

"Me?" Shelby asked. Why would *she* be mad? "No. I . . . I thought *you* were mad."

Ryan kicked at a pebble on the ground and stepped aside to let Dorothy, the Scarecrow, and the Tin Man pass by. "Then why didn't you return any of my messages?" he asked.

Shelby blinked. She was confused. "What messages?"

"I texted, I called . . ." Ryan's eyes widened almost to the size of his round HP glasses. "You never got my messages?"

Shelby shook her head no. "Maybe you had the wrong number," she said softly. She couldn't believe what she was hearing. She'd been miserable for weeks and all for—

"Shelby, let's *go*!" The biggest tabby on the block suddenly grabbed Shelby's arm and started pulling. "We're wasting time. Dad's picking us up at nine thirty, and I only have a quarter of my pillowcase filled. Come *on*!" Juniper yanked again and bumped into Ryan. She stepped back and scowled. Shelby thought it was lucky she didn't hiss. "Who are you?" Juniper demanded.

"Ryan, this is my little sister, Juniper. She's annoying,"

Shelby said through gritted teeth. "And she's going to have to wait a moment." She locked eyes with Juniper and stared her down. Juniper pouted but settled.

"Is that a bat in your jacket?" Ryan asked, ignoring the sister struggle and suddenly noticing Dusty peeking out of Shelby's coat.

Dusty sat up and wagged faster.

"He's a dog! Duh," Juniper blurted.

Shelby shot her another look, and Ryan started in with his explosion of sneezes. "Are you okay?" Shelby asked. Ryan had his face buried in the crook of his elbow.

"That's. A. Dog," he managed to say between sneezes.

"That's what I said." Juniper rolled her eyes. This guy was not too bright.

"I'm. Allergic. To. Dogs." Ryan punctuated every word with a sneeze. "Super. Allergic."

Shelby backed up. "Oh! I'm sorry." She felt a moment of relief. The sneezing fit made sense now! Then she felt the despair rush right back in. She lived on a *dog-training ranch*! Her life revolved around dogs! She would always have something dog on her! "I better get him away from you."

"No, wait." Ryan's sneezing slowed enough that he could get in a few words before each new nose explosion. "It's okay," he said. "Next time. We go to. The movies. I'll be sure to. Take. Allergy medicine." He smiled, red-eyed. "He's cute," he added, pointing at Dusty and backing away.

"Yep," Shelby muttered, watching Ryan go with a dazed smile. "He is the cutest."

16

Pedro approached the canine pavilion, whistling happily. Though he'd missed having Dusty snuggling against him while he slept the night before, he couldn't have been happier about the pup's first assessment. And he also couldn't deny liking the sense of satisfaction he got knowing that his (and Shelby's) hunch about the tiny pup had so far been correct. Dusty was destined for great things, and Pedro felt certain today was the day that Roxanne would officially agree to begin the Chihuahua's training.

When he pulled open the door to the pavilion, his whistling stopped and his lips parted into a broad smile. Sitting on the counter was a large bowl of candy left by the Sterling kids—mostly Juniper, because her sweet tooth was almost as big as his and she always got the biggest trick-or-treat haul. It was well known that Pedro liked *anything* sweet, so they always forked over their "unwanted" candies. Usually he looked forward to the post-Halloween candy bowl for weeks, but he'd been so distracted by Dusty this year he'd actually forgotten. It was a welcome surprise. His pace quickening, he stepped up to the counter and pawed through the fun-sized treats to select a few that would go well with his second cup of coffee.

He was unwrapping a Mounds when Georgia arrived with Roxanne on her heels. "Oh good, you're already here," Georgia said. It wasn't even seven o'clock—they were all up early. "I wanted to talk to you both about Dusty."

Pedro stopped chewing for a second, wondering what this meant. He hoped it wasn't a curveball.

"I couldn't sleep last night because I was thinking about that little pup and how comforting he has been to Shelby," Georgia began, pushing her dark curls over her shoulders. "I absolutely agree that he is special, and that he should be trained. I just wonder if he's meant to be a comfort or service animal instead of a SAR dog . . . if he might be more successful on a service path. Dusty is exceptionally good at comforting humans. Every single one of us has fallen for him." She paused for a breath, but Pedro knew she wasn't finished. Knowing Georgia, she was probably just getting started.

"He's the perfect size to ride in a wheelchair, and he's already traveled on an airplane. He's attentive to humans and could probably be trained as a hearing dog or to help a person with limited mobility, or someone dealing with anxiety or PTSD . . ." She trailed off, as if she had run out of words. Pedro noticed that sometime during Georgia's speech Roxanne had started to nod in agreement, and he sighed internally. Until that moment he'd thought Dusty had convinced Roxanne of his SAR potential, but apparently the little dude had more work to do.

"I hear you," Pedro said, thinking his words through. "We all agree Dusty is special, and I can see how you'd think his size and his personality would lend themselves to therapy or service work. But there's no denying his resilience, determination, and drive, and many of the dogs who have come to us have been trained for service work but end up failing because they have too strong a prey drive or too much energy, or both. We all saw Dusty with that stuffed bear yesterday . . ."

Roxanne's foot was tapping soundlessly on the polished concrete floor. Though she had her doubts, everything Pedro was saying was true. And she could tell that she wasn't going to be able to change his mind about Dusty no matter what she said.

"He did extremely well on the initial evaluations," Pedro added. "I think he has earned himself the right to try a few tracking exercises."

Roxanne's foot stilled and her gaze traveled back to Georgia's face. The more they discussed this, the more it became clear that the only way to know for sure was to keep working with Dusty and see what came of it. "You have some terrific points, Georgia," she said. "But since we don't train service dogs, I think we owe it to the pup to see if he has the skill set for the kind of training we *do* do, and that's SAR work."

Georgia's eyes momentarily flashed disappointment but quickly cleared. She was a realist, and she'd only been making a suggestion. "All right, then, let's see how he does with training and tracking." She smiled. "Thanks to both of you for hearing me out."

"Of course," Pedro replied honestly. One of the things he loved about Sterling ranch was the mutual respect among the people who ran it. Nobody had to be in charge for the sake of power—it was all about the dogs and their potential to help save lives. Everybody understood that nothing was more important than that.

Later that morning, Roxanne took Dusty out to the training grounds for round two. Shelby and Pedro had both wanted to come along, but Roxanne had given them a firm no. They needed Dusty to be as distraction free as possible for this assessment. So Pedro went to a meeting at the local fire department to discuss the possible creation of SAR canine/handler teams, while Shelby followed her siblings out the door to the school bus stop. Shelby was a little disappointed but felt better than she had in a long while. She had been up texting with Ryan for almost an hour before her mom took her phone away. They weren't officially boyfriend and girlfriend, but they were definitely a thing.

With Forrest and Morgan also at school, and a new dog thrown in the mix, Roxanne was short on training help. She reached out to Eloise first. Eloise had worked on the ranch as a training assistant, especially a victim, on several occasions, and had recently applied for the job of assistant trainer.

For canine help, Roxanne chose Radar, a large black Lab who was mid-stream in his training and, for the most part, easy to work with. Radar's only issue was his occasional insecurity. As was the case with many strays, Roxanne didn't know what exactly had happened to Radar before he came to the ranch, but he took several weeks to gain trust and was still a sensitive guy. He needed regular reassurance and plenty of love when he wasn't working. This morning, though, he seemed confident and eager to work.

Out on the training grounds, Eloise left a scent pad—a particular spot laden with her smell—for both Radar and Dusty. Once she was hiding, she radioed Roxanne, who emerged from the pavilion with the dogs. Radar and Dusty made a comical pair. Radar's gait was lumbering and intentional, while Dusty's legs moved so fast the four blurred into one! Dusty was so much smaller than the Lab that two of him stacked on top of each other wouldn't have reached the underside of Radar's belly. Radar wore his red SAR vest, while Dusty wore his mostly white birthday suit. It turned out that Forrest had been right . . . they didn't make SAR vests small enough for the Chihuahua, though Morgan and Shelby were working on a solution to that.

Roxanne brought Dusty over to the shade structure and secured him to the base of the bench. Dogs who had been working with her for a few weeks could be told to sit and stay, but she didn't expect that from Dusty, and she didn't want to set him up to fail. He would be challenged enough this morning already.

"Good boy," she told him. "Stay." Dusty wagged at her as she departed for the middle of the training area with Radar, but his haunches didn't leave the ground.

At the scent pad, Roxanne gave the Lab some positive cues and waited for him to focus on her. Radar set his nose to the ground and inhaled for a good minute, fully waking up his scenting skills and taking in Eloise's smell. When he looked up again, Roxanne gave the command.

"Find!"

Radar didn't need any reminders. His usual lumbering pace shifted into one of purpose, and he traced Eloise's steps, following the trail of skin cells—imperceptible to humans but stronger than stinky cheese to dogs—that she had shed along her path. Within five minutes Radar had found her and was barking the alert. While Dusty wagged and wagged and pulled slightly on his leash, Radar kept barking until Roxanne found him and his "victim." Then he got his reward—a game of tug-of-war with a piece of thick rope knotted on both ends.

While Roxanne led Radar to the shade shelter to

swap out dogs, Eloise found a new place to hide near the rubble pile. Roxanne waited patiently until she felt confident that she was well situated, then introduced Dusty to the scent pad. Dusty, for his part, didn't seem the slightest bit interested. He didn't even put his nose to the ground.

"It's a clue, buddy," Roxanne said. "It's right here. Take a sniff." Dusty looked up at her, his ears pricked high. He didn't seem to be catching on.

"Dusty, here. Smell here."

"Yip!" Dusty replied, but did not lower his nose.

"You're killing me, dude," Roxanne murmured, surprised by her feelings of disappointment. Dusty becoming a SAR dog still seemed impossible to her, but she found herself wanting him to prove her wrong, to show her he had the goods. Roxanne loved an underdog. Literally.

"Yip!" Dusty barked again. He was now sitting right on top of the scent pad and looking up at her *very* intently. "Yip, yip!" Roxanne could sense his eagerness to get to it, so she didn't hesitate any longer.

"Dusty, find!" she said.

Dusty was off like a miniature cannon. Instead of tracking the trail left on the ground, though, he kept his nose in the air, sniffing. He honed in on Eloise's scent quickly and moved fast. Roxanne had to speed walk to keep up! She knew that Eloise hadn't hidden *in* the pile—that would have been too dangerous, even for a dog with alleged agility.

As Roxanne followed Dusty to the rubble pile, she realized her mistake. Eloise had been instructed to hide on the far side of the pile, and Dusty was headed straight for it. The fearless pup was taking the most direct route . . . over and through it!

"Dusty!" she called. He looked *so tiny* as he started to scale the scrap heap. He stopped and turned to her, balancing on a piece of pipe. Roxanne hesitated. This was crazy! But she remembered what the others had said about his agility, and Dusty himself had chosen his route. Letting him take it would give her a chance to see for herself. She took a deep breath, deciding to trust the little dog's instincts. "Find!" she called.

Dusty scrambled up and over the pile without toppling any of the balanced debris. His tiny size really *was* a remarkable asset! He located the rottweiler lady on the far side and started to bark like he'd heard the bigger dog do. No training required!

"Yip! Yip, yip, yip, yip!"

Roxanne made her way to the pair as quickly as she could. She checked her stopwatch for the dog's time, and her own when she arrived. Dusty had found Eloise in an incredible nine minutes, and it had taken her another six to get to him because she had to take the long way around! She gave him a liver treat and pulled Bear out of her bag.

"Yip!" Dusty let out a final bark and spun in circles. He loved Bear. He loved working and finding people. He loved treats!

"He's pretty incredible," Eloise commented with a smile as she pulled bits of debris from her light-brown hair.

Roxanne stared down at the remarkable runt in happy shock. He might have other limitations, but there was no denying that this could easily be the best first "find" she'd ever seen.

17

Pedro sat in his office in the handlers' lodge tapping his fingers on his desk. He'd been working on a new PowerPoint presentation for several hours and was feeling a little twitchy—class prep wasn't a particular strength even though it was an important part of his job. And while his command of English was strong—he was fluent—every once in a while he came across something that he could only explain accurately in Spanish. He rubbed his temples, then sat back and focused his eyes on the photos of SAR handler-and-dog teams who had trained on the ranch . . . a welcome relief. His eyes strayed to the clock on the wall. It was 4:34 p.m., almost quitting time. He needed to wrap things up! If only he weren't so distracted about how his favorite Chihuahua was faring with Roxanne. He gave himself a little pep talk and was returning his attention back to his presentation when three of the Sterling kids burst into his office still wearing their backpacks.

"He's a scenter!" Shelby shouted gleefully.

"An *air* scenter," Morgan corrected. "All SAR dogs are scenters, Shelby." Shelby was so excited for Dusty and in such a great mood that she didn't even respond to being corrected by her little sister. Who cared? In addition to Dusty passing his assessment with flying colors (they had raced straight to Roxanne for the report), she'd sat by Ryan in history *and* lunch today, and he didn't sneeze once!

Pedro sat back in his chair and absorbed their excitement . . . another welcome relief from his PowerPoint. Their jubilation filled the room and mixed with his own. He couldn't help it; he was proud of his former roommate. By the time Roxanne appeared in the doorframe with Dusty on a lead, the small office was positively buzzing.

Pedro raised his chin slightly at Roxanne, smiling broadly. "Tell me everything," he said.

Roxanne smiled back, sheepishly. "You were right, and I should have listened," she replied with a tiny bow.

Pedro threw his head back in laughter. "I didn't mean for you to say I was right," he told her, his dark eyes sparkling. "I just want to hear what happened today!"

Roxanne shook her head, bemused. "Oh, that!" She reached into the bowl of candy on Pedro's desk and chose a strawberry Laffy Taffy. Unwrapping it and popping it into her mouth, she let the anticipation build while she chewed and swallowed.

"Yip!" Dusty let out a bark, as if to say, "Tell them already!"

"I have to admit I was skeptical when we started, and even more skeptical when he completely ignored the scent pad. He didn't lower his nose to it for a single second!"

"Because he didn't need to!" Shelby interrupted.

The corner of Roxanne's lips curved upward. "Apparently not. The moment I gave the command, he ran straight for the rubble pile. I'd told Eloise to hide *behind* the pile, not even considering that he would choose to go *over* it. But that's exactly what he did, and found Eloise immediately."

Pedro raised an eyebrow. "I guess he *really* likes that pile!"

Forrest crouched down next to Dusty and stroked the length of his body along the top of his back. "I misjudged you, lap rat," he said. "You're actually a *rubble* rat!"

Dusty wagged his tail and licked Forrest's hand. He loved having all eyes on him, especially when nobody was laughing.

Roxanne nodded. "He navigated that danger zone with total ease."

Shelby squatted next to her brother to give her favorite pup some love. "Of course he did," she said. "He's like a miniature gymnast." Dusty leaned into Shelby's hand and wagged harder.

"Hadn't really thought about it before, but I can't

actually imagine a better dog for a destruction scenario. Dusty's so light he won't disturb the wreck and make things worse, and he's small enough to fit through tight spaces where humans or even big dogs can't go," Roxanne said, thinking out loud. Then, coming out of her own thoughts, her eyes lowered to Dusty and she kind of snapped to attention. "He will have to learn to accommodate for his size on rescues," she said. "Nontheless, it's official. We're definitely training this little guy to be a SAR disaster dog."

"Yessssssss!" Forrest said.

"Woo-hoo!" Morgan added.

Shelby lowered her face to Dusty's and whispered her congratulations, her heart squeezing. "I guess that means he can't be my lap dog anymore," she said.

Roxanne shook her head in agreement but understood Shelby's sadness. Before she'd become a trainer, she'd adopted a stray who, though she didn't know it at the time, was destined to become a SAR dog. Saying goodbye to their life together was bittersweet, to say the least. She reached down to touch Shelby's shoulder.

"No, I'm afraid he can't. Little Dusty has big things to do." She paused, tapping her foot on the floor. Thinking. "But I *will* need a training assistant. Shelby, since you were such a believer in Dusty's skill, the job is yours if your parents agree."

Morgan's head swiveled in Roxanne's direction while frustration started to bubble up. She knew it wasn't fair and tried to swallow it back. But until Dusty showed up, Shelby was one hundred percent over anything having anything to do with dogs!

Shelby straightened, her face alight. Just as quickly, though, her expression dimmed as if a cloud had passed over it. More time with Dusty would undoubtedly mean more allergic reactions for Ryan. Plus, being involved with his training would be like watching him get closer to leaving the ranch, little by little, day by day. It might just be too much to take. Shelby crossed her legs on the floor and pulled Dusty into her lap. She put her face close to his fur. Her siblings, Roxanne, and Pedro watched, fully aware of the situation and what it meant for Shelby. She was as attached to Dusty as Juniper was to Twig!

Shelby held her nose against the soft white fur on Dusty's neck for several long moments, letting the smell of him act as a balm for her conflicted soul. Dusty nestled under her chin. Words weren't necessary.

Finally Shelby set Dusty on the hardwood floor and stood up. She shook her head. "I think I should stick with my job in the welcome center," she said, sighing. "Maybe Morgan can take my place."

Forrest scowled at his oldest sister. Technically Morgan was too young to train with the dogs . . . *he* was supposed to be the lead "kid" assistant. But he knew better than to object—it wasn't his decision, and he couldn't deny that he *did* spend the last month teasing Dusty about his, um, shortcomings. He just didn't see the tiny pup's potential—he was too focused on his size. Lesson learned.

Morgan blinked, a bit confused. Was her sister actually handing her a training job . . . one of the most unusual ones the Sterling Center had ever had?

Her heart soared with excitement. This was basically a dream come true!

"Yip!" Dusty spoke up, and it brought Morgan back to earth. This was only an *idea*, one her parents had to get behind . . . especially her mom.

"I'll talk to your parents, Morgan, and see what they say," Roxanne said.

Morgan felt hope rise again. Roxanne seemed fully on board, and her opinion generally carried a lot of weight. Maybe, just maybe, she would get to train the brilliant Dusty after all.

18

Morgan stepped on a twig and nearly jumped out of her skin. She was sneaking through the dark with her headlamp set to its lowest setting and was, to be honest, a little spooked. The moonless sky hovered over her in pitch black, and she had to keep her headlamp on the creepiest setting . . . red. She'd only gone prowling around the ranch at night by herself once, and it hadn't exactly ended well. At least this time it was sanctioned.

Her mother had agreed to let Morgan help Roxanne train Dusty, and tonight was the first nighttime training. They'd been working with Dusty for over a month, and the Chihuahua was proving to be a very fast learner. They'd started with finds during the day, at first nearby and then with Morgan hiding farther and farther away, with more and more of a time delay. Continued barking during alerts was also a breeze for him, and his re-finds and returns to Roxanne went well, too. The latest joke around the Sterling dinner table was that for a dog with such a tiny head, he sure had a big brain!

"His brain is probably in his ears!" Forrest had said with a laugh. And Morgan half agreed with him. It seemed there was nothing this dog couldn't do.

Snap! Another stick broke under her foot, and she silently hoped that Roxanne and Dusty were still inside so the dog wouldn't hear it, though it wouldn't surprise her if he could hear through walls!

Since this was Dusty's first try at night training, Roxanne had told Morgan that she could hide pretty much wherever she wanted on the ranch, but that it shouldn't be too *hidden*. They wanted to make him work but also make her relatively visible since there wouldn't be any light. Morgan crept past the second shade structure and kept going until she arrived at the newest addition to the ranch . . . the bus wreck. She'd only explored it once briefly, and that was during the day. She was surprised by how much larger and more menacing it seemed at night. Tipped on its side, it really did look like it had just crashed. Being careful not to step on the glass from the blown-out windows, she made her way around the far side to one of the upturned front wheels. She took a deep breath, settled in, and turned off her headlamp. The dark wait had begun.

Back inside the canine pavilion, Roxanne strapped Dusty into his tiny vest. Morgan had searched online until she found the smallest vest available. Then Shelby had adapted it to Dusty's little body with her sewing skills and the Sterling Center's industrial sewing machine.

"Nice fit," Roxanne said with a smile as she checked to make sure the straps were snug. Dusty let out a bark but continued holding perfectly still. He liked his new wardrobe and wanted to make sure it was adequately admired!

When they were both ready, Roxanne and Dusty

stepped out of the canine pavilion and into the dark. Dusty wore a small light that Roxanne had secured to his collar. This was more for herself than for him— dogs could see better than humans in the dark, but it was difficult for humans to see them. After adjusting her own headlamp, Roxanne turned the setting to red so as not to distract the dog more than necessary.

Night training could be tricky. Some handlers preferred to keep their dogs close when on a night search, while others let them range as if it were daylight. Since Roxanne had no way of knowing the preference of a dog's future handler, she generally took a middle-of-the-road approach and kept the dog from ranging as far as he or she naturally would during the day. This almost always achieved a balance that worked.

The moment they stepped outside, Roxanne noticed that Dusty seemed uncomfortable. His antenna tail drooped, and he didn't carry himself in his usual proud stance. He stopped walking multiple times before they even got to their starting point at the training grounds. It wasn't like him.

"It's okay, Dusty," she told him. "It's the same ranch, just without the daylight and hot sun." Dusty eventually came along, but he didn't demonstrate the excitement or enthusiasm for training she was used to seeing. Roxanne had to force herself not to worry along with him—she had to stay neutral, to send the message that everything was a-okay, perfectly normal. The last thing she wanted was to heighten his uneasiness.

Dusty's heart thrummed rapidly in his chest. There was no wind. There was no moon. The light attached to his collar bobbed around, casting spooky shadows. He wanted to go back to the doggy castle, to his cozy bed or the trailer or Shelby's lap. He wondered why he was out at night.

Roxanne led him to the usual starting place. She held out a piece of clothing for him to smell, but like always, he ignored it. He already knew the smell he was to follow—knew it by heart. It was Morgan's smell.

Dusty had found Morgan many times a day for

many days. He usually started searching for her late in the day, when the sun was far across the sky, but sometimes he tracked her all day long. She was good at hiding, and he had to search in lots of places. But this was the first time Roxanne had asked him to find her at night. He had never been asked to work at night, and he didn't like it. Night reminded him of hunger. Of fatigue. Of the family he lost.

"Dusty." Roxanne's voice was stern. She wanted him to focus. Dusty stilled and looked up at her. She held his gaze for a long time. Then she said the word: "Find!"

Dusty sniffed the air for Morgan and got her scent in his snout. He knew right away where she was, but he didn't want to go there. He didn't want to leave Roxanne's side.

"Dusty, find!" Roxanne repeated. She didn't sound angry. She sounded patient, and very serious.

Dusty started out but stopped with one paw in the air. Fear was getting the best of him. He circled back. He tried again, and circled back again. Out and back. Out and back. He looked up at Roxanne. His body felt tense and his tail drooped. He knew he wasn't doing what he was supposed to do, but he couldn't make his feet take him to his target. Not in the dark!

"Find Morgan." Roxanne tried a new tact. There was worry in her eyes.

Morgan. Dusty heard the name and it gave him a tiny burst of courage. He left Roxanne's side again, and this time he got his legs to keep going. He passed the shade shelter and the doggy castle. He made it past the rubble pile. His light was still bobbing around and his heart was still thrumming, but his legs moved him toward the smell, toward Morgan.

Roxanne looked at her watch as she followed, closer than she knew she should. Already it had taken Dusty a full twenty-four minutes, more than four times his daytime rate, and he hadn't made it to the target. Half that time was spent just trying to get him to start the search. By the time he zeroed in on Morgan's hiding place next to the bus wreck, his tail was fully between his legs. During the final approach his body was so low to the ground it was scraping dirt. Roxanne was tempted to call him back, but full-on failing might only make things worse.

"Yip!" Dusty barked tightly when he was next to Morgan. "Yip, yip, yip!"

"That took forever!" Morgan said as soon as she spotted Roxanne.

Her assistant looked nearly as spooked as Dusty and sounded relieved that the search was complete. "I was worried!" Morgan confessed.

Roxanne looked down at the still-cowering Dusty, thinking that if she had a tail it would be between her legs as well. If Dusty was unable to work at night, there was no way he could earn his certification. There was no way around it. For the first time since she'd agreed to train him, Roxanne felt worried. "Me, too, Morgan," she said. "Me, too."

19

The sun was beginning its descent in the hazy blue California sky when Luis Cortez turned the wheel of his Dodge pickup and pulled into the parking lot of the Sterling Center. He'd been driving for several hours and needed a bathroom break ASAP. San Antonio, Texas, was not exactly right next door, and his back and legs were reminding him that he was no longer a spring chicken ... more like an aging rooster. Still, he was glad to be here. The more miles he'd put behind him, the more certain he was that taking this trip was the right decision.

Retirement from the police force had not exactly gone the way Luis had imagined. He'd thought he'd take up fishing in addition to his regular poker games, and enjoy having time to read and hike. He planned to visit his brother more frequently in Mexico. He'd had no idea that the slow predictability of his days would gradually drive him bonkers. Who knew retired life would be one monotonous day after another? It wasn't exactly that he missed working on the force. He'd put in his time and was ready to be finished with the grind and the toll of police work. As a cop you never knew what was coming around the corner, both literally and figuratively. Retirement was just, well, boring, and also a little bit lonely. Like it or not, the folks on the force had become a family to him, and he missed being around them every day. He missed the community. So when a friend suggested he get certified to work with a SAR dog and join a unit, he said he'd think about it. And the more he thought about it, the more he liked the idea. Joining a search and rescue unit would (1) allow him to be part of something bigger than himself, (2) allow him to help out when needed, and (3) give him a constant companion to boot. Before he knew it he was researching possibilities and looking for places to train. The Sterling Center came highly recommended, so he'd contacted Pedro Sundal a month ago. After a phone interview and an application process, here he was.

The young lady behind the desk in the welcome center recognized a desperate bladder and directed him to the restroom the moment he walked through the door. When he returned she was waiting with a handshake and a warm welcome.

"You must be Luis Cortez," she said. "I'm Shelby Sterling. We've been expecting you." The girl couldn't have been older than fifteen or sixteen, but her handshake was firm and she looked him right in the eye. Luis liked her on the spot.

"I've just told Pedro Sundal that you've arrived. He should be here any—"

The door swung open and Pedro appeared, smiling and with his right hand already extended. Luis noticed that his handshake was also firm. That made two for two.

"Welcome to Sterling ranch" Pablo said. "Bienvenidos."

"Mucho gusto. Gracias." The two men clapped each other on the back like they were old friends, Pedro reaching up because Luis was a big man. The two began speaking in easy Spanish and were still carrying on when Pablo led Luis out of the welcome center for the usual introductory tour. Shelby waved them off with a smile, wondering which dog Luis would be paired with. He seemed to have a personality as big as his physique.

Luis followed Pedro all over the ranch, happy to have a chance to stretch his long legs. He could tell right away that the Sterling Center was a fantastic place. He was especially excited to see the shepherds and Labradors and golden retrievers and border collies in the canine pavilion, and wondered which of the big dogs he was going to be partnered with. He was itching to find out!

At the end of the tour Pedro led Luis to the handlers' lodge. "This will be your casa for the time being," he said, showing him the kitchen, the common space, and his room. "The bathrooms are down the hall, and our classroom is at the end of that hallway."

"How much of the training did you say is in the classroom?" Luis asked, passing a hand over his bald head and feeling a bit deflated for the first time since he'd first arrived. Classroom work had never been his thing, and after nearly three decades on the force and five years with the canine unit, how much was there left to learn?

"Two weeks," Pablo replied, sensing Luis's lack of excitement. "I think we do a good job breaking it up with reading, presentations, and videos. We really try to keep it interesting."

"Classwork? Interesting?" Luis's voice was full of doubt. "Just to be clear, I'm no newbie. I've got a lot of experience with emergencies and trauma and dogs."

Pedro was careful to listen, to make sure Luis felt heard. It was as important to build trust with the human handlers as it was with the dogs—maybe even more so. "De verdad, Luis," Pedro said. "I believe you.

I am sure some of the material will be review, but it's always good to refresh your memory and expand knowledge. Disaster training is different from police work, and it's often the things you don't realize you've learned or that you thought wouldn't matter that save the day in the field."

Luis felt a small wave of frustration but didn't push. He'd signed up for the program and was determined to see it through, classroom work and all.

The two weeks were a bit of a slog, but Luis liked the other handlers he was learning with, Holly and Jake. They were both smart and no-nonsense. And he had to admit he was learning a lot more than he thought he would. Who knew that dogs could be so sensitive to a handler's mood, or that some dogs preferred a tug-of-war reward to liver treats? Every dog he'd ever met was a sucker for any kind of food . . . sort of like he was. Even though the information was sometimes fascinating, classroom learning was as much of a challenge as it was when he was in the police academy, and he found himself nodding off more than once.

Still, it was worth pushing himself to concentrate. Every day he told himself he was one day closer to meeting his canine partner. Meeting his dog was the thing he was most excited about, by far, and it kept him going.

Finally meet-and-greet day arrived. Luis awoke early and had too many cups of coffee even though he had more than enough energy to begin with. He had to make several trips to the bathroom. After a hearty breakfast that Holly and Jake seemed to linger over forever, it was time.

"Are you ready?" Pedro asked when the dishes were done.

"About to burst," Luis replied honestly.

Pedro led the handlers out onto a field with wooden bleachers at one end. In the near distance, three gorgeous dogs were lined up obediently with lead trainer Roxanne, proudly wearing their SAR vests. Luis could see a border collie, a golden retriever, and a sturdy black Lab. Luis grinned from ear to ear, feeling a wave of happy satisfaction. All three dogs looked fit to work with him, to get the job done, and he was about to be partnered with one of them!

They walked closer until they were about twenty yards from the dogs, and turned to face them. The border collie strained at his leash, but then settled obediently at Roxanne's side. The three handlers were fidgety as well. What were they waiting for? Why wasn't the woman calling them forward?

"Yip!" came a punctuating bark from behind them.

The handlers all turned to see a young girl approaching with the most ridiculous dog Luis had ever seen . . . a Chihuahua mix with insanely large ears. The minuscule dog's legs moved so fast Luis thought there might actually be more than four! He laughed aloud. "What is *that*?"

Nobody answered him, and the girl, who he could now see was Morgan—the middle Sterling daughter—was walking right toward the handlers and Pedro, and then Pedro was reaching out a hand and taking the leash. The coffee in Luis's stomach began churning uneasily.

Pedro turned to face Luis directly. "Luis, this is Dusty," he said. "I think the two of you would make a great team."

The coffee threatened to revolt. "Dusty, as in . . . *dirt*?" Luis blurted, his jaw tight. He felt humiliation wash over him. Why on earth would Pedro want to match him with a dog who could be blown away by a stiff breeze? The mutt was so tiny his vest didn't even look like the other dogs'!

"Yip!" Dusty's bark was sharp—he would not be brushed off.

Pedro felt a pinch of disappointment. Not only was Luis's reaction not positive, it was full-on negative. He wasn't surprised, however—he'd been expecting this. But it wouldn't be long before Dusty had a chance to prove himself . . . and he only needed one.

"You might not believe it now, but this is the only dog on the ranch with enough machismo and confidence to match you," Pedro stated. Morgan was nodding her agreement.

Luis wanted to throw up his hands in refusal and storm away—he was that upset. But something held his feet to the ground, and he forced a laugh. He would see it through. He'd put a lot of time and energy into his training, and Pedro had shown himself to be smart and knowledgeable. He knew what he was doing. Luis swallowed and looked down at the runty dog. Ugh. No! Okay . . . fine. He'd do a test run with this little runt to show Pedro that they were a terrible fit.

Dusty gazed steadily up at Luis. He could feel the new man's reluctance, and it fed his determination. He would *not* be underestimated!

After handing Dusty off to Pedro and Luis, whom Morgan was not particularly fond of at the moment, she headed over to join Roxanne and Forrest. It was lucky that today was Saturday and they could help with the various scenarios Roxanne was going to throw at the new teams. Plus, Morgan loved matching day! Seeing the dogs, who had been working so hard for so long, finally meet their probable partners was almost always amazing. Not every match stuck, but the dogs usually knew which person was meant to be theirs.

It took just a few minutes for Radar to connect with Holly. Her patient, reassuring nature was perfect for the Lab, and he seemed to gain confidence just being near her. The border collie, Telluride, took to Jake quickly, too. They were both brimming with energy and would be able to keep up with each other, no problem. For now, the golden retriever called King would remain on the sidelines, but it wouldn't be long before he, too, found a partner. Luis gazed at the large blond dog longingly as he lined up with Dusty beside the other pairs.

Roxanne had asked Forrest to be the victim for one of the exercises, while Morgan was there to provide an extra set of eyes and ears, observing how the teams worked together. Conferring with Roxanne and Pedro was a new job for her, and an honor. She felt proud to know the trainers trusted her powers of observation. She had already noticed Luis's skepticism, of course. It was obvious to all.

"Good thing Shelby isn't here to see this guy doubting Dusty," Forrest whispered, leaning in close to her ear. "She'd be furious!"

"No kidding," Morgan agreed. But she also, reluctantly, understood. She'd had her initial doubts about the pup, too . . . before she knew him.

The first task was for the dogs to take a trial run on an agility course that Martin and Forrest had set up the night before. Roxanne had the handlers lead their dogs through the canine obstacle course. One by one the dogs had to make their way over slippery pipes, across teeter-totters, across a large, angled section of chain-link fencing, and up ladders. The dogs had been trained for this, and Roxanne knew they could complete the tasks, though she still held her breath each time Dusty jumped from ladder rung to ladder rung. What they were watching for was how the dogs performed with their potential handlers. Did they listen? Did they respond? Was there chemistry? In a nutshell, did the handlers help or hinder the dogs?

Radar was first and aced the course in no time. His only stumble was on the ladder that crossed a galvanized tub of water. He slipped but righted himself quickly and made it across. He finished the course in seven and a half minutes.

Telluride also did well, finishing in just over eight minutes.

Luis's body language was not what Roxanne and Pedro would have hoped for. His arms were crossed over his chest, and he kept looking at the big dogs instead of focusing his attention on Dusty, who sat patiently at his side.

When it was Dusty's turn, Luis almost winced in anticipation as the tiny dog approached the first obstacle. Then his jaw dropped when the little dog sped into a full run and leaped onto the end of the teeter-totter, landing perfectly and balancing for a mere nanosecond before crossing it, jumping to the ground, and moving on to the long, horizontal section of chain-link fencing. Luis watched in amazement as the little pup managed to grab hold of the narrow links of fence, never once letting a paw slip through. On the ladder he had to jump from rung to rung because he was so small, but he moved quickly and landed securely every single time. It was the same on each obstacle, and he finished the course in six minutes.

Dusty trotted dutifully back to Luis. He looked him in the eye and sat down at his side but did not accept a treat. The Sterling gang had to stifle a collective laugh. You had to hand it to the Chihuahua—he had hutzpah!

Luis raised an eyebrow, suddenly doubting that the golden retriever could have completed the course so well.

"Okay, Forrest, you can head out," Roxanne called to the boy. "You know where to go." Forest nodded and left to hide in a cluster of trees halfway to the bus wreck.

Though all the dogs were well trained, the human-canine teams were brand-new. It took time for working pairs to learn to trust each other and perfect their communications, so today they would keep the searches simple.

The search order was the same, and the results were nearly identical. All three dogs performed well, but Dusty bested the big dogs by more than a minute. Luis was flabbergasted and once more Dusty barely accepted his praise. He knew he was good—and he was going to make sure Luis knew it, too.

While Morgan, Roxanne, and Pedro watched, Luis

lowered his large frame all the way to the ground. He waited patiently for Dusty to approach. Dusty took his own sweet time. When he finally reached his new partner, Luis lowered his head in respect.

"Dusty, I had you all wrong," he admitted softly. "You're more SAR dog than the rest of these mutts combined."

Dusty stepped closer and sat down next to Luis, almost touching. He lifted his tiny snout and sniffed the air, then looked at the big man beside him.

"Partners?" Luis asked, extending his hand.

Dusty gave it a lick and held his head up proudly as Pedro approached. The human trainer struggled to keep his grin at bay. He could see that a bridge had been built—and crossed—for both of them. Luis and Dusty understood and respected each other.

"I think you're right," Luis admitted to Pedro, taking the toothpick out of his mouth. "This is my dog."

20

Luis wiggled his habitual toothpick between his front teeth as he approached the canine pavilion, where he knew Dusty was waiting. It had only taken a few days for Luis to understand that patience was no easier for the pup than it was for him—they were both impatient creatures. It was one of the ways in which they were similar, and knowing this helped them to understand each other as they progressed through the training.

They'd spent the first three weeks almost solely at, in, and on the rubble pile, where Luis continued to be amazed by the little dog's skill, fearlessness, and grace. He was almost like a canine hovercraft—it appeared he barely touched the pipes, broken boards, and pieces of concrete he had to navigate. His issue, the one Roxanne was helping them work on now that they seemed to have conquered his night fears, was that he was such a natural he often moved *too* quickly. Though this rarely got him into trouble during training because of his skill, Roxanne felt strongly that he had to temper his inclination to move fast all the time. Rushing could be extremely dangerous in a disaster. She spent three long, tedious days having Luis make him back up and cross a single pipe over and over (and over), until Dusty doubled the time it took.

Luis, for his part, felt like an elephant in a tulip garden whenever *he* had to get onto the pile. Every step required balancing and adjusting, and he tripped and fell so many times his body was covered in black and blue. Little by little his skills (and his respect for Dusty's) improved, and he was able to move a bit more quickly. And, as Pedro reminded him, in the actual field Dusty would be the real searcher . . . the handler's job was mostly about staying clear, making good decisions on the fly, and giving commands to keep the dog safe. That, and staying mentally strong.

"Disaster work is some of the hardest and most dangerous SAR work there is," Pedro explained. "Both you and Dusty will need to be fleet and sure, and, perhaps, most importantly, comfortable working and making decisions independently. There will invariably be unstable structures, hazardous materials, confined areas . . . and loss of life. You will be dealing with tragedy on almost every call."

"Physical strength and stamina will be essential," Roxanne had added, as if Luis weren't already a bit overwhelmed. "But I can't say enough about the importance of *mental* strength, and the ability to stay flexible. You will face long days and nights and brutal physical and emotional situations. You might find a live victim but not be able to get to them because it's not safe. Or you might get someone out alive only to have them die at the hospital. And that's if you find *anyone* alive . . ." Her pale face was grave, her green eyes shadowed with past and future trauma. Luis actually wondered if she had lost someone in a tragedy herself.

"It's just the nature of the beast, I'm afraid," Pedro said solemnly.

Luis knew this, but hearing it out loud made him swallow hard. He'd never actively participated in disaster work, but fairly early in his police career he'd offered his rescue services after an explosion at an oil refinery off the coast of Texas. The conditions had been horrendous. There had been much loss of life—human and sea creature—and the thick coating of crude oil was dangerous and had a sickly smell that lined everyone's noses and stuck to them for weeks afterward. When Pedro told him that he and Dusty were signing up for some of the most grueling work there was, he didn't need to be told twice.

More than once since he'd arrived at the ranch, Luis had questioned his decision. Part of him was mentally and physically wiped out from his years on the force. Part of him wanted to be done. But he'd tried that, hadn't he? And he'd been bored and lonely and maybe even a little depressed. It hadn't worked.

He pulled open the canine pavilion door, telling himself he'd made the right decision, like he did most mornings. And also like most mornings, seeing Dusty solidified this belief. The pup was standing at the door to his kennel wagging like mad. As Luis approached he let out a single, ecstatic bark. "Yip!"

Inside his little body, Dusty was barking more than just once—he was barking and barking and barking, because seeing Luis every morning was the best! It meant they were going to work, and he loved work! And he loved Luis.

When Dusty first met him, he could tell that the man didn't want to be his partner—that he doubted he could do the work. Dusty could see it in his body language. He could smell it. But that very same day Roxanne had all the dogs doing searches, and Dusty was good at searching. Really good. It didn't take long for Luis to see *how* good. The big guy hadn't doubted him since. And he'd also taken him out to the rubble pile to work every day since.

The rubble pile was like a giant playground that required extra dexterity and skill to play on. Dusty loved climbing around, balancing, and sniffing out the teensy-tiny spaces. He loved leaving the big dogs in the dust as he steadied himself in each unstable spot or squeezed through the smallest cracks. After his time on the streets searching for food and hiding from danger, there was something almost comforting about searching in confined areas. And since the rubble pile was always changing, it never got boring. Dusty had a knack, and now that his tummy was always full and he had a safe place to sleep, he could give training his all.

The anxious yips wanted to come out, but Dusty swallowed each and every one. Keeping his barks inside came at a cost, though . . . his back end wiggled a little bit extra. Beaming down at him, Luis let him out of the kennel and scooped him up. This was their ritual—a moment of being held and scratched behind his nicked ear. After that, Luis always put Dusty down and let him navigate whatever came their way on his own four feet, the way the pup liked it.

"Ready to get to work, tough guy?" Luis asked. Dusty gave Luis several licks in reply, each one a clear "Yes!"

Out by the rubble pile, which had just been carefully readjusted by Martin and his machinery, Roxanne was getting ready for the day. It was a big one! She felt an unusual wave of anticipation as she saw Luis and Dusty approach, and even started giving them instructions before they'd stopped walking.

"You two are doing so great that we're going to throw you a couple of curveballs today," she announced, her arms gesturing to the pile. "I usually take this one step at a time, but Dusty is unusual, and my gut tells me he can handle a lot of this stuff at once."

She opened her pack and took out what looked like four tiny red sacks with Velcro near the top. "We had to have these custom made, so I hope they work."

"Are those booties?" Luis asked, unable to hide his surprise.

Roxanne nodded and bent to slip the first one on. "You never know what kinds of hazardous materials disaster dogs are going to encounter, so they've got to tolerate protective gear. Let's see how Dusty does with these . . . and how you do, too." She secured the booty and stood to hand the other three to Luis. Luis wanted to laugh but knew better. Biting his tongue, he bent his broad back and slipped a booty onto Dusty's left hind leg. It was harder than it looked! There wasn't a lot of extra space, and he had to secure it snugly but not so tightly that it cut off the pup's circulation—Dusty would certainly need to feel his feet! Once he got the hang of it, though, the other two booties went on more easily. Dusty was extremely patient.

After all the ointment and socks he'd had to wear while his feet were healing, he accepted the close-fitting booties like a champ.

"And these," Roxanne said, reaching into her messenger bag and pulling out some protective eyewear. "Doggles."

This time Luis bit his tongue so hard he was physically unable to utter a single syllable. They looked ridiculous, but he had to keep it cool for Dusty. He maintained a serious expression while he slid one strap under the Chihuahua's chin and the other behind his ears. They fit snuggly, so they wouldn't catch on anything.

Dusty, miraculously, didn't try to paw them off. He just blinked through the clear lenses. And now that the pup was wearing them, Luis realized how hardcore they made him look. Heck, they were probably bulletproof!

"You *know* you look good!" Luis said with a giant grin.

"Yip!" Dusty replied, as if to say, "Heck yes, I do!" Luis could have sworn he was standing a little taller, too.

"That's not all," Roxanne said as Luis's nose wrinkled. He'd gotten a whiff of something unsavory . . . something he suspected had to do with whatever Roxanne was about to tell him. Dusty's nose quivered, high in the air. He clearly smelled it, too. Luis was about to ask *what* else when he noticed that Roxanne's attention had shifted to the rubble pile behind them. Turning, he saw that they had more folks than usual helping with training—a lot more. He could see at least five people on or around the massive heap, including the three oldest Sterling kids. His eyes settled on Shelby, and worry tugged at his chest.

"Won't it be a distraction to have so many people around?" he asked. They both knew that Shelby was his biggest concern—she and Dusty had a special bond.

"That's actually the point," Roxanne explained with a nod. She adjusted her trucker's cap, her green eyes alight with anticipation. "Today we start proofing."

"Ah," Luis replied. He'd learned all about proofing in class with Pedro. Proofing was about presenting the dog with as real a disaster situation as possible, so that the dog learned to ignore everything he or she wasn't actually searching for in a disaster . . . everything but live human beings.

"We're adding more people, strange smells, strange sounds. We're gonna throw it all at him and see if Dusty can stay on target. In a real disaster there will be loads of distractions—things we can't even begin to anticipate."

Luis nodded. He understood just how important proofing was—he just never thought they'd throw this many things at Dusty on the first go. Luis knew his dog was special, but this would be a challenge for sure.

Dusty, for his part, was getting used to his new gear. The goggles made everything seem a little squashed, but they weren't as irritating as the footwear. He stepped gingerly from paw to paw, trying to adjust to them. The booties made his paws feel kind of numb, like they weren't fully attached to his legs. It wasn't fun. Chewing them off sounded waayyyyy better. Much more fun, and a good challenge! But he knew Roxanne and Luis had put the footwear on for a reason. The fact that they put them on meant that they were supposed to be there. So he sat down on his haunches and lifted his nose to the air.

There were some loco smells swirling around! There was *always* a lot to smell on the ranch—humans, dogs, food, trees, dirt—the rubble pile alone smelled like about fifty different things. Today, though, there was even more. He sniffed again and again. The new smells were making him eager to get to work! He walked over and sat down next to Luis and looked up at him, signaling that he was ready to roll.

"All set?" Roxanne asked.

"Always," Luis replied with a nod. He lowered his gaze to Dusty. "Find!" he commanded.

Dusty did not need to hear the word twice. He took off like a shot, heading for the rubble pile, turning left and skirting the edge. His nose buzzed with the myriad of smells. He raced roughly halfway around, taking them in and listening with his giant ears. Somewhere not too far away someone was using a chainsaw. The loud *raarrrr raarrr raarrr* made Dusty's ears twitch, and the smells of gasoline and wood and grease burned his nostrils. Part of him wanted to pause, but he knew he wasn't supposed to. None of those smells had anything to do with his target.

He trotted forward, then stopped when one of his favorite smells grabbed his snout. Shelby! He smelled

Shelby, and he loved Shelby! Shelby smelled like kindness and enchiladas. Shelby's lap was warm and cozy and the perfect size. Sheeelllbyyy!

Shelby was not his target.

Dusty's nose twitched. The smell of Morgan was right behind the smell of Shelby. Dusty loved Morgan! She gave him food every morning. She picked up his poop. She hid for him a *lot*!

Morgan was not his target, either.

Dusty's target was hidden in the pile, and he was getting closer. He trotted forward a few Chihuahua lengths and leaped onto a broken piece of plywood, then ducked under a crumpled piece of chain-link fencing. He scrambled up a massive chunk of cement before stepping onto a pallet that teetered beneath him. He paused, shifted his weight, and continued on.

"Good dog," Luis called when the pallet stilled and Dusty continued up the pile.

Suddenly Dusty's nose started to quiver in a new way. He smelled something he'd never smelled while on a search. Food! Even after being fed regularly for months, the smell of food still tantalized him. His brain still told him to *find food find food find food*, and his legs desperately wanted to respond. He stopped and sniffed. Took a step forward. Stopped again. And again. The meaty scent of canned dog food swelled into his snout, making him drool right there on the fat PVC pipe he was standing on. His nostrils widened. He swallowed the saliva. He licked his lips.

Dusty was not supposed to find food when he was working . . . nunca. Not ever. He held perfectly still. He took a long, indulgent sniff. Then he turned away from the dog food smell and picked a careful path around to the far side of the rubble pile. Here there were a lot of pipes in all shapes and sizes—some skinny, some fat, some straight, and some twisted. Some set off wafts of metal, while others smelled of plastic. Something lured him into a wide steel pipe. The sides were slippery, but the smell coming from the far end of it was loco strong: rotten chicken!

Back before he came to the ranch, Dusty would have gulped rotten chicken down in a second and suffered for it a couple of hours later. Not today. Not now. He was working. As stinky good as it was, the chicken was not the target, either. He crawled back out of the pipe.

"Yes!" Luis cheered. He'd been pacing on the ground next to this section of the rubble pile, keeping an eye on Dusty from a distance. Now he shouted encouragement. "Find!"

Not too far away, Forrest was banging rebar on rebar. It was really, really loud. Dusty scampered away from him, over some shiny flashing metal and broken concrete. He followed his nose, ignoring the smell of a rat coming from behind the broken drywall. Normally enticing, but not today. Not his target.

Sniff. Sniff. Sniff. More quivering. He hadn't smelled *that* smell since his days of picking through gas station garbage cans. Dirty human diaper! Kind of delicious, kind of disgusting. Dusty was getting a teensy bit impatient. So many smells were assaulting him, but none of them were the right smell! None of them were the *rottweiler lady*!

But wait! Dusty stopped. He sniffed again at the delicious disgustingness. There was something mixed in with it, and he needed to check out what it was.

Yes! It was the smell he'd been sniffing for. At last! Stifling a bark of excitement, he commando-crawled under a plank of wood. The plank was longer and lower than he expected, and he had to press his belly to the ground to get through. Finally he could smell that he was *there*—he was in the right place. The rottweiler lady and the dirty diaper were *both* on the other side of a big piece of plywood. *Now* was the time to bark.

"Yip!" Dusty alerted Luis. "Yip, yip, yip!" He barked and barked and barked but didn't dig. He knew that digging on rubble piles could cause problems.

"Incredible," Roxanne said as she and Luis approached. "I've honestly never seen a dog that was anything like him."

Dusty puffed out his little chest, beaming with pride, and so did Luis. "He's an original, all right," the ex-cop crowed as he stuck a fresh toothpick between his front teeth.

"He's got a laser focus not usually found in strays." Roxanne was still shaking her head as she and Luis pulled aside the board that concealed Eloise and the stink bomb.

Eloise stepped out, gasping a little and fanning her pale face. "I can't believe you made me hide with a *diaper*!" Her blue eyes were laughing.

Roxanne patted her on the shoulder and grinned. "Look on the bright side," she joked. "You just significantly increased your chances of getting hired full-time at the Sterling Center!"

21

Shelby groaned, rolled over, and slapped her alarm clock into silence. Why did seven thirty feel so much earlier on Saturday than it did on Thursday? She would have liked to close her eyes and drift back to sleep. There was only one thing that could make her get up this early on a weekend. Okay, maybe two. But the one she was thinking of was black-and-white and had enormous ears and would be leaving the ranch today. No way was she going to miss her chance to say goodbye to Dusty.

Even though she hadn't been getting the lap and cuddle time she used to—not since November when Dusty started training, and she and Ryan became a thing—she'd taken comfort in the fact that he was still on the ranch. And she'd visited him whenever she could. But once he received his certification he'd be leaving for Texas with Luis. And Shelby was going to miss him like crazy.

"Ugh!" Shelby groaned again and sat up.

"Are you going to be okay?" Morgan asked, pulling her head out of their shared closet. She knew today was going to be hard for her big sister.

"I'm just really going to miss him," Shelby whined.

Morgan pulled a flannel shirt off a hanger and buttoned it on, coming over to Shelby's bed.

"He's probably the best listener I've ever met," her sister finished.

Morgan finished her buttoning and nodded seriously, then smirked. "Well, with those ears he oughta be," she quipped. But it didn't get a crack of a smile out of Shelby. She was too bummed.

Morgan knew exactly what her sister meant, and how she felt. Some dogs were fantastic listeners. Over the years Morgan had told dogs plenty of things she wouldn't tell anyone else. She couldn't totally explain it, but the right dog had a way of making you feel . . . heard. Understood. Better.

There was nothing Morgan could say to make Shelby feel better. Dusty was leaving, which was great and also really, really hard. So she just squeezed her sister's hand in support.

"That little dog sure has big pull!" Frances looked around the training field at the crowd that had gathered to watch the demonstration and certification ceremony. Certification was a big deal, and it didn't happen every day. Today three dogs were hopefully going to get certified and move on. But despite the fact that they were incredible dogs with many skills, the crowd wasn't there to see Radar or Telluride. They had come to see the mighty mini mutt: Dusty.

This situation had been brought about in part because Georgia recognized a good publicity moment. She'd alerted the media about their tiny graduate by sending out press releases and making a call to her friend at the local radio station. A notice about the ceremony had been in the local paper, and a guy with a TV camera was there to capture some cute footage for the evening news. Frances saw a couple of other people she suspected were reporters, too, and Pedro's niece, Sylvia, was a sought-after interviewee once the word got out that she had been the one to rescue Dusty from a trash heap on the side of the road.

Sylvia, for her part, was thrilled to be there. She'd driven up from school with Xander to see Dusty "graduate" and start his new life—and to meet his human partner, Luis.

Roxanne surveyed the scene, appearing cool, calm, and collected on the outside. Inside she felt a little like jelly. She was used to having a few observers at certification demos, but there were at least fifty people here—a bigger crowd than the dogs had seen before. She spotted Frances, taking her own survey of the scene. Roxanne suspected the older woman felt a strong sense of pride . . . this was, after all, her making.

Just then Frances looked in Roxanne's direction and caught her eye, giving her a satisfied and supportive nod. It was exactly what Roxanne needed. It made her realize that she felt pride, too—that her trainees had all been proofed and were up to snuff. The dogs were ready, and so were their handlers. Looking over at the bright-eyed, wagging pups standing beside their people, she saw that for them this wasn't nerve-racking in the least—it was fun!

Radar was first, and Roxanne shot a video of him on her phone. The hesitation and trust challenges he'd struggled with were nowhere to be seen. He moved with confidence and appeared unflappable. When the crowd applauded at the end of his course, he ate it up like a bowl of peanut butter, completing a victory lap with his tail held high.

Telluride loved the audience, too. He put on a little extra speed during the second half—just enough to get through the course half a minute faster but not so fast as to risk losing control—and when he finished he ran in tight circles, spinning like a top before grabbing the length of fire hose that was his favorite toy and giving it a good shake.

But Dusty! Roxanne had to work hard to keep from laughing when her teensy trainee was up. He swaggered to the middle of the course with his chest puffed up in his red vest, totally aware that all eyes were on him. Luis walked beside him, equally puffed, and the pair stood side by side and waited for Roxanne's cue to start. When Roxanne nodded, Luis gave Dusty a hand signal and the Chihuahua mutt was off. He practically floated through the agility course, his feet only touching down occasionally. He ran through a string of commands with Luis with such intense focus Roxanne wondered if they were communicating telepathically! And when it came time for scent article searching (the dogs had to locate a hidden handkerchief loaded with human smell), Dusty blew the big dogs away. It wasn't a competition, of course, but nobody could tell that to Dusty. He strutted around the field waving the handkerchief like a victory flag. The crowd loved it.

Roxanne, still recording with her phone, panned over the faces to catch their reactions. Frances, Martin, Georgia, and Forrest were all grinning ear-to-ear. Morgan, Juniper, and Shelby were standing close together. The two older girls had their arms linked tightly, and though they were all smiling, too, Shelby's eyes glistened with tears. The folks from town clapped and laughed and nudged one another. Pedro stood with his niece and Xander. Sylvia's mouth hung open in disbelief. Pedro looked like a proud papa, and when Roxanne caught his eye, she gave him a nod of excitement and gratitude. Pedro had understood early on that Dusty was up for anything, and together they'd prepared a fantastic team. Roxanne felt ready to burst herself!

With a gulp, Roxanne stepped into the middle of the field and made the certification announcements. She called the teams up, one by one. They were official now and it was time for the dogs to leave the ranch, to go train with units near their new homes. It was time for them to get down to the rewarding and challenging work of being SAR dogs. Certification days were always the happiest and saddest at the center, and today was no exception.

22

Dusty stood in the parking lot surrounded by people and wagged. The big crowd that had cheered for him on the field was mostly gone, and now the faces hovering over him were familiar. They were his favorite faces, and they made him wag even faster. Looking up at the kind smiles, Dusty barely remembered a time when he did not like people.

Sylvia, the human who had pulled him out of the ditch, was the one who started this big shift. She had cared about him when there was no one else to care, when he was totally alone. He remembered how he had shivered in her sweatshirt, too stunned and scared to think.

"I knew you could do it!" Sylvia said, kneeling down. "I knew you were something special." Dusty let her scratch him behind the ears, then rolled onto his back so she could get his belly. He was grateful for this girl and would be forever. She had brought him to this place, this dog heaven. The ranch was where things had really changed for him.

Pedro squatted down, too. "You know I can't resist that belly!" He laughed. "Gonna miss having you around, big guy," he confessed in a low voice tinged with sadness.

Dusty didn't know what Pedro was saying, exactly. But he could smell his sad mixed in with his tantalizing aroma of Flamin' Hot Cheetos.

Pedro stood. Dusty did, too, shaking off the dust. He shook so hard his feet came off the ground, and a second later he was scooped up into a warm pair of arms.

Shelby held the little dog high, close to her face. Dusty licked her cheek. Shelby was so sweet to him. He thought of the time when his feet were sore and his stomach was churning and Shelby held him in her warm lap day after day. It was the perfect place to get better. He licked her cheek again. It was wet and tasted like salt.

The other girls, Morgan and the one who smelled like cat, gave Dusty kisses on his head. Then the boy did.

"Good luck, rubble rat." Dusty wagged slowly. "Rubble" was a word he knew. He was good at rubble.

"I'm afraid we need to get on the road," Luis said, interrupting the petting and kissing session. His voice was softer than usual. "Dusty and I have a long drive in front of us."

Shelby nodded. She pressed her forehead to Dusty's snout. She smelled sadder than Pedro. Not the same kind of sad she'd been when he sat on her lap months ago. This was a different sad, and Dusty thought maybe it had something to do with him.

"I will miss you like crazy," Shelby whispered. "But I know you'll be happy." With a last kiss she handed him over to Luis, who set him down on the ground to stand on his own four feet.

Morgan gave Bear to Dusty, and he carried him in

his mouth to Luis's truck. The tall man opened the door and invited Dusty to climb in. He'd put a crate inside, with two cozy blankets. Dusty took a running leap and hopped up onto the seat. He sniffed the crate and dropped Bear inside, then jumped up to the top of it so he had a full view out the windshield. Luis smiled and nodded. "A copilot, not a passenger," he said. "I get it." He closed the door, leaving the window open a crack for some good outside air, and got into the driver's seat.

The Sterling family and trainers, Sylvia, and Xander stood together waving as Luis backed the truck up and rolled toward the parking lot exit.

Everyone watched the retreating truck . . . except Shelby, who couldn't bring herself to look.

"Shelby," Morgan said in a low voice as the truck disappeared. She tugged her sister's hand, but Shelby shook her head and didn't raise it.

"I think you have a visitor." Morgan's voice was insistent. "And I'm pretty sure this will make you feel better."

Finally Shelby raised her head and saw Ryan

walking toward them. He'd never come to the ranch before—he'd never dared. His dog allergies were terrible, and Shelby was certain that being in proximity of this many dogs would land him in the hospital, unable to breathe! She was glad to see him, *super* glad, but . . .

Shelby blinked back her happy/sad tears and put up her hand, signaling to Ryan that it wasn't safe to approach. Ryan, though, wasn't slowing down. He was speeding up with his arms out, going in for the hug.

"I'm covered in dog hair!" Shelby protested.

Ryan wrapped his arms around her, anyway. "I knew this morning would be rough for you," he said, squeezing her. "So I took extra-strength allergy meds as soon as I woke up."

Shelby felt his comforting arms around her shoulders and melted a little. He wasn't a furry creature with white fur and giant ears, but he was pretty awesome.

Ryan pulled back and smiled at her. "Now why don't you show me around this place before the pills wear off?"

23

During his months of training, Dusty had been in several cars. He'd even ridden in a helicopter! But this trip with Luis was the longest ride of his short life. At first it was exciting. With the window open, green smells wafted from the rolling hills, and fields of blossoming trees shared their sweet scent. And the cows! Cows *really* smelled. And underlying it all were the familiar odors of asphalt and rubber and fuel. He tried to take it all in from the top of his crate, sitting up straight and looking around. After a while, though, it got hard to sit. His hindquarters started to ache. So he curled up, still on top of the crate. He watched Luis chomping on the little stick he always kept in the side of his mouth. Luis loved his tiny stick the way some dogs loved big sticks . . . the way Dusty loved Bear. It was funny that a big man liked such a tiny stick. But then again, he liked a tiny dog.

Dusty's eyelids grew heavy. He let them slide closed, even as the smells still drifted into his snout. The smells changed as they drove. Soon the green smells were gone, replaced by the scent of sand, lizards, fast food, and wind.

When he awoke it was dark. Luis was still driving, chewing his stick and singing softly along with the radio. He slowed the truck until it stopped. Dusty stood and stretched, yawning with his tongue out.

"Welcome to Arizona, Dustito!" Luis said. "We're just passing through." He opened the door and the smell of diesel and rubber wafted in on a wave of warm air. All around them Dusty could see the hulking shadows of big, big trucks. They were as big as the bus that killed his pack. He poked his nose out the door. He had to pee, but he did not want to get out.

Luis patted his leg and Dusty jumped down. The

ground was still warm from the day. He lifted his leg on the front tire.

Luis laughed. "Not on *our* tires, dude!"

Dusty didn't respond. He just wanted to let it all out and hop back in the cab as soon as possible!

Luis went inside the big, brightly lit building and came back a few minutes later with a hamburger. He ate it on the tailgate. Dusty sat close, in case of drips, and because the warm dark night was making him quiver. It smelled like danger and loss. It reminded him of the shaky dog he used to be.

"This is our hotel for the night," Luis told him when he'd finished eating. He crawled into the covered back of the truck. There were blankets and pillows and the ground was soft. Luis had made a cozy bed for them.

"Just gotta catch a little sleep," Luis said. "Then we'll get back on the road." He yawned and closed his eyes. Within a few moments, Luis was making a deep growling sound in the back of his mouth and throat. It wasn't angry, though. More like a purr.

Dusty turned on the pillow next to Luis's head. He

circled three times and finally lay down. He closed his eyes and let out a long breath. Still, sleep took a long time to find him. The traffic zooming nearby made him shudder. When he finally dozed off, his eyes flicked beneath his eyelids. They had to move fast to follow the dream images of blowing trash and speeding cars. He whimpered in his sleep, reliving the time when danger was everywhere. When his stomach gnawed at him constantly. When he did not know where his next meal or place to sleep was coming from.

Luis awoke when Dusty started yipping and twitching beside him. He reached an arm over and laid it gently on the pup's soft, warm body. He knew the little guy was having nightmares and wondered, not for the first time, what his life had been like before he'd made it to the ranch. It was a wonder the small dog had survived—he was remarkably smart and tougher than he looked.

But now, Luis worried that Dusty, haunted by his past even in sleep, might not be as bold off the ranch. Something seemed to be changing. The farther they drove, the more his bravado seemed to be overshadowed by something else . . . something traumatized and afraid. He kept his open palm on the pup, practically covering him with it, until he settled.

Luis rolled over, wondering if he'd made a huge mistake. Doubts crept into his thoughts, and not just about Dusty. He had his own doubts, too. Some of his bluster was just that: bluster. He talked big, and hoped that when push came to shove, he'd come through. That was how he rolled and so far, for the most part, it had worked for him. But he wasn't one hundred percent certain that he'd be able to pony up when he and Dusty were in a real crisis situation. He wasn't sure that he'd have the courage and the know-how to power through, and not just during the disaster work, either. He was also concerned about *after*.

Seeing Dusty reshaken by his past since he'd left the ranch reminded Luis of the emotional repercussions of the work he'd chosen for himself long ago, and again more recently. The difference was that now it wasn't just about him . . . it was about Dusty, too. PTSD—post-traumatic stress disorder—and depression were very real consequences for disaster teams, just as they were for soldiers and first responders. His retirement from the police force came at a time when his job was starting to get to him. Being pummeled with danger and constantly having lives on the line had produced cracks in his facade. Luis had been witness to too many stories without happy endings. For years he'd been fine, then one day it was too much. He stopped sleeping well. He wasn't always hungry. He'd had to leave the job he loved. So why had he chosen *this*—a return to the unknown and traumatic—not just for himself, but for the tiniest dog in the world?

Luis heaved a heavy sigh and forced a laugh. "Because you're loco," he whispered to himself. He looked at Dusty, sleeping soundly now, and somehow felt better. They didn't have to do this alone . . . they could do it together. "Maybe we're both just crazy enough," he whispered, and rested his hand on Dusty's small body.

24

The next day the drive was even longer. Or at least it felt that way to both Luis and Dusty after their short night and fitful sleep. By the time they finally crossed the border into Texas and pulled into Luis's drive-way, they were both fighting to keep their eyes open.

"We're here, Dusty," Luis said. He was relieved to see his peach stucco house with its red tile roof just as he'd left it. "We're home," he said, opening the passenger door.

Dusty hopped down, took a long leak *not* on the tire, and lifted his nose in the air. He followed Luis to the front door and inside.

"Home" was a word he'd heard before. Pedro used

to say it a lot, and though Dusty had lived many places, none of them had been a real home, a forever home. Not until now.

"Check it out," Luis said. His voice was happy. "Sniff everything!" He laughed, rubbing his bald head.

The house was small, barely bigger than Pedro's trailer. It was cozy like Pedro's trailer, too. And, in fact, it *smelled* a little like Pedro's trailer—like soup, candy, laundry soap, and bread. But Luis's house smelled a little stale from having been shut up for months with nobody living in it while he'd been in California.

Luis opened a window to circulate the air, and Dusty sniffed the dry breeze. There was none of the pine scent he'd gotten used to on the ranch. There were fewer grassy odors, too. But he loved the new smells of sandy soil and blooming wildflowers mixed with cactus and coyote. He breathed deeply.

"It's not much, but it's all ours," Luis said, motioning around the house. Dusty let out a happy bark, relieved to be off the road. He jumped onto the plaid couch. It smelled of Luis—one of Dusty's favorite new smells. Luis flopped down beside him. "We're going to need to go get some food, but first things first," Luis said, kicking off his boots. "What do you say to a little nap?"

Dusty curled up beside his partner. He hadn't run much in two days—stuck in the cab of the truck—and his legs were restless. Still, he was exhausted and a nap was just what he needed. A nap, at home.

"Yip!" Dusty barked at the dark crack between the counter and the stove. "Yip!" he barked again. He needed Luis's attention. And strength. He had to get back there. Right. Now.

"I'm coming, I'm coming!" Luis called from the bedroom.

Dusty sat down to wait. Settling into life in Texas in the little stucco house had been going well. Dusty had staked his claim to the recliner in the living room, the big pillow in the bedroom, and had marked every stick, bush, tree, and rock in the surrounding area . . . announcing his arrival to the neighborhood dogs and coyotes. He had also conducted a thorough "house cleaning."

"You're better than a vacuum cleaner," Luis had told him after he had licked up every crumb in the place. Well, almost every crumb.

"Yip!" he barked again. Finally Luis emerged from the bedroom. He cocked an eyebrow at the little dog.

"You're really gonna make me move that thing, huh?" he asked, flipping the toothpick in his mouth and crinkling the edges of his eyes.

Luis bent down and grasped the stove on both sides. With a grunt he slid it out of the gap in the counter. Behind the heavy appliance were at least five years' worth of dust bunnies . . . and a single Cheerio.

Luis's laugh boomed as Dusty scampered into the dust and scarfed up the tiny circle of ancient, stale cereal.

"Was it delicious?" Luis asked, still cracking up. "I can't even remember the last time I had Cheerios!" Dusty wagged a thank-you while Luis grabbed a broom and dustpan. "As soon as I'm done back here we'll get to work, okay?"

Luis's worry about Dusty, himself, and what he had taken on had faded since they'd landed at home. With Dusty here, Luis's days felt fuller. Richer. They walked and trained and ate together daily, and slept in the same bed every night.

As soon as they'd gotten back Luis had put in some calls, looking for a SAR disaster unit to work with. He'd gotten in touch with a group nearby that had been working together for a year but could use another canine team. "We'd love to meet you," Luis told the woman on the phone. All he had was a voice to go on and the woman's description of her team, but it had felt like a good fit. Now that the day they were to meet had arrived, Luis was surprised to find himself feeling a little nervous.

Dusty watched Luis getting ready. The big man looked at himself longer in the shiny glass than usual. He chomped down harder on his tiny stick. He changed his shirt twice. He smelled . . . nervous. And it rubbed off. While Luis fussed, Dusty walked in circles near his feet. He nearly whined, wondering what was going on.

"I'm like a kid on the first day of school," Luis said, shaking his head. He knelt down and waited for Dusty to flop over and show his belly. "We've got nothing to worry about," he told the pup, though he knew there was a lot on the line. It was important that a disaster team get along and function well—the group needed chemistry. The right mix was essential when your purpose was to work together in perilous situations.

Luis took Dusty's leash and vest down from the hook by the door. He put it on and tightened the straps. Dusty instantly stood up straighter, making Luis grin. "How could anybody resist you, big guy?" The words made him flash back to *his* first reaction to the Chihuahua, and he quickly pushed the memory out of his head.

25

Dusty balanced on the edge of the truck seat and craned his neck to see out the window. They were not driving to the spot where Luis usually liked to train—a big park with plenty of places for him to hide scent articles. They weren't driving to his friend Bruce's house, either. Bruce and his house smelled like Tater Tots, which Dusty loved.

No, this was a new spot. And it smelled tantalizingly pungent!

"Phew!" Luis fanned his face. "I bet you love that, don't you?" Dusty's fast-moving tail was all the answer he needed as they rolled past the sign for the county landfill. Luis glanced at his notes and went left, away from the place where people were paying to drop off their loads of garbage. He circled an area covered in what appeared to be construction waste and slowed when he saw four cars parked close together. A woman wearing a bandana tied like a kerchief on her head spotted them and waved the truck over.

"Bet that's Laura," Luis said. She was the person he had spoken to on the phone. He'd told her all about his training at Sterling, and how he'd found his perfect canine partner. What he hadn't told her was that his partner was smaller than a Thanksgiving turkey . . . more like the size of a Sunday chicken!

Dusty shifted his paws on the seat. Luis could tell by his panting and the fact that he was looking around more than usual that the Chihuahua was picking up a little of his own anxiety. He took a deep breath and decided he needed to reverse that. Time for them to find some calm, and some courage!

"Hello!" Luis climbed out of his truck with hand extended. "You must be Laura."

"Yes, and you must be Luis," Laura countered and shook his hand before patting her leg twice. A large black Belgian Malinois appeared at her side. "This is Fredo," she said, petting the top of his head without bending over. He looked like an all-black German shepherd with higher hindquarters, and Luis had heard that the breed made great search dogs. Laura cast a glance over Luis's shoulder. "I guess I should have told you to bring your dog," she said, looking a touch confused.

"I did." Luis patted his leg, and Dusty was there in an instant.

Neither Laura nor Fredo could contain their surprise. They both stepped back. "This is . . . ?" Laura started to ask, the words not quite coming.

"This is Dusty," Luis finished for her as the dogs began to circle and sniff.

"But he's . . ."

"A Chihuahua. Mixed with something else, I think. Maybe superhero." Luis winked, not giving Laura a chance to ask anything else. "So, are you going to introduce us to the rest of the team?"

Laura blinked twice and then gave her head a little shake. "Of course! You said you got your certification at the Sterling Center, right?" she asked as they walked over.

Luis offered to show her their papers, but Laura only nodded and smiled. "I just never expected . . ."

"Nobody does," he admitted.

The rest of the disaster team was standing around a pile of pallets that doubled as a table for their coffee mugs and backpacks. Laura introduced them in pairs. "This is Sabrina and Thor," she began. Luis shook hands with a serious-looking woman in her forties and gave her large German shepherd a pat. And this is Paul and Homer. Homer, a very rosy golden retriever, was already on his way over to greet Luis. He offered a paw before Paul could shake Luis's hand." In less than two minutes the dogs were circling and wagging. Their people watched, amused by the new micro-recruit. Dusty didn't have to bother going around to get to the backside of the bigger dogs—he just strolled around underneath them all, weaving in and out of their legs, taking his time to sniff all the information he needed.

"Wow," Paul said. "I've never seen such a small SAR dog. You think he can keep up?"

Luis could tell that despite his upbeat tone, Paul wasn't so much impressed as incredulous. His askew eyebrows revealed that he didn't think Dusty had what it took. And he wasn't the only one, either. Luis caught all of the handlers exchanging glances when they thought he wasn't looking. There was only one way to squash their doubts, he realized. And that was to show them what Dusty could do.

"Okay!" Laura clapped her hands to call everyone to order. Once she had their attention, she went over the standard operating procedure, or SOP. They were going to treat this exercise like a real disaster. That was the best way to see how they would work together. It was important to make sure that everyone and every dog was up to the task.

"I'll be acting as Incident Commander, based right here. Fredo will stay with me," Laura explained. She spread out a map on the stack of pallets, and Luis saw that it showed the large landfill area. "I've marked off the areas where we're allowed to go." The city was generously allowing them to use part of the landfill for training. Outside of Sterling, it was hard to find a real simulated disaster scene west of the Mississippi. The bulldozed piles most closely resembled the landscape they might find after an earthquake, hurricane, or tornado. Only the smell and the seagulls wheeling overhead reminded them it was a dump.

"The victims are already hidden in the designated areas, and I've asked them to hide themselves completely. They've been out here since seven a.m., so they're probably getting a little tired of being buried in trash."

Each team took a two-way radio, and Laura assigned them quadrants. Whichever team cleared their quadrant first would take the remaining quarter.

Luis walked to the edge of the area he and Dusty had been assigned. He tried to imagine that it was a neighborhood after a storm, that there were living people in the tower of garbage. Dusty bounced beside him, anxious to hear the *clink* of his leash being snapped off. Finally Luis stopped. He stooped and removed Dusty's leash and entire vest. The garbage mound had many small openings, tunnels, and protrusions . . . Dusty would be safest without anything that could snag.

Dusty stared up at his partner, trembling with excitement. The best part was—

"Go search," Luis commanded.

This! Dusty scaled the scrap heap like a seasoned pro, his ears on high alert, his nose on overdrive. This new search area smelled like nothing he had ever sniffed before, and his nose was stuffed with it. Plus, there were lots of dark nooks and crannies for him to poke his snout into or crawl inside to inspect. He understood that "go search" was different from "find." His job was to smell for a person, any person. He was waiting to hear a movement, a breath, a heartbeat.

"Yip!" It did not take long. "Yip! Yip! Yip!" Dusty's small bark traveled back over the distance he had covered, all the way to Luis. He kept up the alert until Luis had traversed the trash heap and was standing beside him. It was a tough walk, and though he had practiced hard and gotten much better at navigating rubbish piles, Luis arrived out of breath with muck on his shoes and pants.

"Yip!" Dusty told him again. He nosed a board

buried in junk. There was a person behind it. He was sure.

"Here?" Luis asked. He radioed Laura. "I have an alert," he told her. "Confirming." Then he unburied the board enough to lift it and a red-faced woman with white hair wearing a garbage bag like a rain poncho crawled out. She looked at Dusty with a sparkly expression, not batting an eye at his size. Luis practically wanted to kiss her. "Am I glad to see you!" she told him.

Luis pulled Bear from his jacket pocket and let Dusty tug and chew on him while he radioed confirmation to Laura.

"You two can start on the last quadrant. The others are still looking. Fast work, Luis!"

Luis silenced the radio. "She means you, Dustito." He held out his hand so Dusty could return Bear. Dusty cocked his head. "More searching," Luis explained.

Dusty dropped Bear and wagged. Sometimes he wasn't sure what he liked better—a good tug or a good search.

When they got to the last quadrant and Dusty heard the words he always waited for, he lifted his nose and made a long arc in front of the debris. He paused and raised one paw. He filled his nose again. Then, without a second's hesitation, he began to climb.

Nearby, Thor barked the next alert. His bark echoed in the landfill, deep and loud. Luis listened in on the radio as the second victim was confirmed found. "Two down," Luis said to himself. He wanted Dusty to show them all up. He wanted Dusty to be the best! He'd found the first victim. That was something. But would it be enough to convince the others that Dusty was talented enough for the team?

"Yip!"

"Or you can go ahead and find another!" Luis resisted pumping his fist as he tackled the pile and located Dusty on the far edge of their second search area. Dusty was barking and wagging and wearing a doggy grin, just as excited as Luis.

Shifting a large piece of sheet rock, Dusty's second victim emerged, and Luis called it in.

"Great work," he told his partner, who chose to lie

down in the debris with Bear secured in his teeth. His latest victory called for a high-quality chomp session, pronto! Dusty chewed happily on Bear's ear while the victim and Luis took turns petting him.

After Homer had barked *his* alert, they gathered around the pallets to celebrate their success with the coffee that was left in Laura's big plaid thermos and a box of donuts that Paul pulled out of his station wagon.

"Welcome to the team," Paul said, holding his glazed pastry up to "toast" Luis's maple old-fashioned.

Luis beamed and touched donuts.

"The rock stars have arrived," Laura crowed. "I don't know why I ever doubted you, tiny wonder." She reached down and scratched Dusty behind the ears. Dusty wagged. He kept Bear clamped in his teeth to remind everyone of the fun game, and how he'd won.

Only Sabrina still looked a little reluctant about the new recruits. Sensing that she was accustomed to being top dog, Luis broke his donut and offered Sabrina half. She took it with a smirk. "Consolation prize?" she asked.

"Think of it as a team win," Luis suggested.

Sabrina laughed. "You know he's exceptional, right?" she asked, cutting her eyes toward Dusty . . . who was still flaunting Bear.

"Yeah," Luis admitted. "And he knows it, too," he added in a whisper.

Sabrina stuffed the half donut into her mouth. "Okay, then," she said, still chewing. "I can get used to consolation prizes. Welcome to the team."

26

Luis's ringtone crept into his dreams. The beeping played on the edges of his consciousness for several minutes before finally waking him up. "Huh. What?" he muttered, coming around and fumbling for his phone. He looked at the glowing numbers before pushing accept and saw that it was 4:54 a.m. Who would be calling him this early?

"Hello?" he said, unable to keep the early-morning frog out of his voice.

"Luis? It's Laura."

Luis sat up fast. Of course! Laura was the person who would be calling at five a.m. This was it—the call he'd been waiting for, the call he'd half hoped would never come.

"There's been an earthquake, a seven-point-eight, in Mexico."

Luis's heart began pumping fast and hard, making it difficult to absorb everything Laura was saying. The back of his neck prickled. He was from Mexico, and his brother and his family still lived there. "Where?" he half demanded.

"Puebla," Laura replied.

That didn't exactly answer Luis's question. Puebla was a state, a municipality, *and* a city. Six million people lived in the state, and a million and a half of them made their home in the city of the same name. He'd grown up in a big family in the state, but in a smaller town northwest of the city, in the place where his brother still lived.

"The city, or the municipality?" he asked, trying to hone in.

"Municipality. Outside the city. We're still finalizing our target location."

The hairs on the back of Luis's neck were now

standing straight out. His brother, Paco, and his family could be in danger. He told himself to calm down, to not borrow trouble. What were the chances the quake was close enough to have impacted their town?

Luis paced his small bedroom, any lingering sleepiness gone.

Dusty was wide-awake as well, sitting attentively on Luis's pillow. His eyes were locked on his person, and his big ears twitched as if he could hear *and* understand the conversation that was happening on the phone.

"We're mobilizing soon," Laura said. "I'll call you back with travel details. Keep your phone on you, and charged."

"Absolutely," Luis agreed before hanging up. He immediately tried to call his brother at home but got a recorded message reporting that all circuits were busy. He tried his cell phone, too, but couldn't get through there, either. He sent a text saying he'd heard about the quake and asking if he and his family were okay.

Just heard about the quake. ¿Están bien?

He considered adding that he and the San Antonio SAR team were being dispatched to help, but decided that information could wait. He sat back down on his bed, closed his eyes, and mumbled a silent prayer that Paco and his family were all right. ¡Por favor!

"Yip!" Dusty fidgeted uneasily. He could tell that something was worrying Luis. The big guy only closed his eyes sitting up when something bad had happened. He felt comforted when Luis opened his eyes again and reached out an arm to pet him.

"We aren't going to borrow trouble, right?" he said aloud. Dusty had no idea what he was saying but let out a second bark in reply.

Within a moment Luis was on his feet again. He threw his bed into its usual form of made and went to the closet to get out his gear. He kept a backpack and a duffel ready to go for moments like these, but there were always things to add—namely sustenance for both him and Dusty. He added dog food, nuts, jerky, and a few apples.

Dusty watched his partner go back and forth from the kitchen cupboards to the backpack he'd placed on the table, his ears following him as much as his eyes. He could tell from the backpack that they were going on a rescue. He could also tell that Luis was anxious. The smell of worry wafted off him. Dusty sat at his feet while Luis added the food items and water to his pack. Now and then he gave Luis's ankle a comforting lick, and once his shiny head when he bent to pick something off the floor.

When he ran out of things to stuff into his bag, Luis sat down in the kitchen chair. Dusty jumped into his lap and Luis pet him distractedly. "It's not good, Dusty," he said. "It's not good."

Once he was dressed, Luis realized he didn't have anything more to do except wait. The minutes ticked by agonizingly slowly. He checked his phone for a reply from his brother, but there were no new messages and he didn't want to tie up the circuits any more than they already were.

"Yip!" Luis raised his head and saw Dusty sitting next to his food bowl, tail wagging. He'd forgotten to feed him! And himself, for that matter. Not that he was hungry. Still, he knew it would be just plain estupido to allow himself or his dog to be deployed on empty stomachs. So he filled Dusty's bowl with kibble and got out a carton of eggs and some bread for himself.

While he ate he switched on the radio to listen to the news. There was not a lot of information coming out of Mexico, but what was reported was bad. Heavy destruction. Towns flattened. People trapped. Thousands missing. And now fires were starting to burn.

Luis checked his phone again. Still nothing. The eggs in his stomach started to churn. He got out his laptop and combed the Internet for more information. Several news sites were reporting on the earthquake, and all sounded equally pessimistic. He found a map showing where the epicenter was and swallowed hard. It was less than ten miles from his brother's village. He called Paco again, to no avail. He sent another text. His leg bounced like a needle in a sewing machine, moving up and down frantically. He realized that the toothpick in his mouth was nothing but splinters.

Luis got to his feet and paced. He consulted his packing checklist and unpacked and repacked the duffel to make sure he had everything. Twice. Part of him wanted to get in the car with Dusty and start driving south, but he knew that wouldn't be a smart choice. He also knew he should probably tell Laura about his brother's family being close to the epicenter. But what if she wouldn't let him go?

Dusty watched Luis's face and smelled his worry. The moment Luis sat down he crawled into his lap and licked his hand. It calmed them both, but Luis could not stay seated for long.

"I'm worried, Dustito," Luis whispered, absently stroking his fur. He didn't have to say it. Dusty knew. It was as obvious as skunk spray or a forgotten can of beans in the back of the fridge.

Finally, around 9:10, Luis got a callback from Laura.

"It's time to head to the airport," she said. "All eight of us are booked on a flight departing in two and a half hours. I'll see you there."

Luis hung up the phone and ran his hand over his head. It would still be hours and hours before they'd arrive, before they could start helping. But at least they were ready to get moving.

Dusty didn't mind the flight. It reminded him of the airplane ride to the States with the woman who saved him, only this time he didn't feel nervous or scared. He felt ready to work! He also felt warm and cozy snuggled together with the other dogs being dispatched—Thor, Homer, and Fredo. Their human handlers were seated in the four-seat first row, and the dogs took up every last inch of floor not commandeered by human feet. And even though the other passengers weren't allowed to pet them or give them treats, they still got a lot of attention. Dusty loved attention!

The only problem, really, was that it was hard to comfort Luis from the floor. He couldn't curl up in his lap or lick his hand to remind him that they were in this together, that it was going to be all right. He hoped Laura, Paul, and Sabrina were helping him with that.

The moment the plane touched down Laura got into the business of logistics. "We've got to get to the Enterprise rental counter," she said. "Normally we'd be escorted there, but the dispatcher I spoke to this morning was spread so thin I told her we could manage."

"Follow me," Luis said. "I've been to this airport a million times."

The Mexico City airport was busier than usual, and it was always bustling. Throngs of people rushed to get to immigration and baggage, and then through customs. The dogs and their vests helped the SAR unit get to the front of the line. Everyone was worried about the earthquake, the damage, and the missing people. Seeing a crew heading out to help gave them hope.

"Thank you for coming!" the immigration officer said in English. Her smiling eyes landed on Thor and Homer and then Fredo, but her brow wrinkled in confusion when she spotted Dusty. "Why is that dog wearing a vest?" she demanded.

Luis sighed and prepared to pull out Dusty's certification papers, but Laura held him off.

"Believe it or not he's our lead rescue dog," she said, meeting the woman's gaze.

The woman raised a penciled eyebrow but said nothing more. She just stamped all the passports and let them through, watching them go, aghast.

After collecting their baggage, the team got through customs and headed to rental cars, which required a shuttle bus ride. By now Luis felt like his whole body was twitching. He looked at his phone every two minutes. Nothing.

Dusty and the other dogs basked in the points and stares of everyone they passed.

The woman at the Enterprise rental counter gave them the biggest van she had . . . but with four people, four dogs, and their rescue gear, they needed two. It took an agonizing fifteen minutes to track down a suitable second vehicle. Luis put a fresh toothpick in his mouth and flipped it over and over with his tongue in an effort not to chomp it to bits.

"I am so sorry," the woman kept saying. Luis could tell that Laura's unuttered response was something along the lines of "Tell that to the people trapped beneath rubble a hundred miles from here," and admired her reserve. She just said, "We need a vehicle as quickly as possible. Any vehicle."

Luis used the extra minutes to send another text message. He even tried again to call—maybe now that they were closer the circuits wouldn't be as busy. No such luck. The recording played again. Luis took a handkerchief from his pocket and mopped the back of his neck where the hairs were still standing on end.

Finally the eight Texans, people and dogs, piled into two vehicles and started the drive, which would take as long as the flight, if they were lucky. It was rush hour, and the streets and highways were clogged with cars and trucks—some trying to get to the site of the quake, some trying to flee the city, and still others just trying to get home from a day at work.

Luis drove the lead vehicle, with Laura taking the wheel of the second. While the other dogs slept,

Dusty sat in Luis's lap, looking through the steering wheel to the windshield beyond. The side window was cracked open a tiny bit, and familiar and strange smells reached his nostrils. Food, asphalt, metal, engines, and people. Lots and lots of people.

Luis tried to focus on the road and not the shifting landscape as they drove. Once they left the main highway, though, their speed was drastically reduced, and it was impossible not to see the destruction. Each town they passed was worse off than the one before. Shops and casitas and hole-in-the-wall restaurants had collapsed in on themselves, sometimes leaving the tables and chairs intact. Smoke lingered in the air from the fires that followed the quake. They seemed to have been put out—at least right here. Luis knew that fires were a terrifying result of earthquakes—damaged gas lines often erupted into flames that did more damage than the shaking itself.

As they approached the epicenter, the damage was more and more devastating. Whole buildings had collapsed. The road was crumpled in places.

They had to drive carefully and sometimes go around places where the asphalt had buckled. In some places road crews had done emergency repairs so essential vehicles could get across. The setting sun cast this horror in a beautiful pink glow, almost making it look like a museum photo or a movie set. It was surreal and creepy. It would be dark soon, and lights wouldn't turn on. Power wouldn't be restored tonight. It could be off for days, or weeks.

All in all, it was hard to grasp what they were seeing.

Luis gulped and reached a hand to stroke Dusty's soft fur, thinking of his brother, and realizing that every last bit of what he was seeing was real.

27

Finally, just after last light, the two vans crawled into the town of Aztecan. Luis checked his phone the moment the engine was turned off . . . nothing. His instincts told him to go to Paco's house immediately, but he also knew he wasn't here as an individual. He was part of a crew, and his job was to help the larger team with their rescue efforts. He wasn't here for his brother or his brother's family. He was here for the earthquake victims—all of them. He was here to search.

Shoving his instincts aside, he focused on the efforts of the group. The problem was, it wasn't entirely clear what those efforts were, because chaos ruled. Most of the streets were broken, buckled, or blocked by building debris, fallen trees, or both.

"I need you all to stay right here," Laura said. "I'm going to see if I can find someone in charge." Luis nodded, looking over Laura's shoulder and noting a human chain of people moving rubble out of the street with their hands to let a fire truck pass. Farther down the block—or what he guessed was a block, since it was impossible to tell where one block ended and another began—makeshift tents and shelters had been set up to house and feed displaced people. Anyone could see it wasn't enough.

Dusty sat sniffing the air, his fur and ears lying almost flat. Somewhere nearby he could smell food, but it was a tiny smell compared to the smell of metal and broken concrete and crushed wood and blood and death. Those smells clogged his nose, refusing to make room for anything else.

"I think that's the medical tent," Paul said. Homer sat patiently by his side, ever calm and steady. They'd heard that the town's medical clinic—small to begin with—had been flattened, and further destroyed by fire. They silently took in the scene. Each of them wondered how much help they could possibly be. The situation was overwhelming. Luis bent down and picked up a rock from the road and carried it to the edge. One stone at a time, they would clear up the mess.

"Paul, Sabrina, over here!" Laura called. "I found the staging area."

The dogs and their handlers picked their way around a pile of rubble to Laura and followed her to a large tent lit by emergency lights and a generator on wheels. Laura didn't waste a second. She introduced them to the Incident Commander, a man named Julio. Julio's English was slow, so Luis spoke to him in Spanish and translated. The look Julio gave Dusty, though, didn't require *any* language.

Luis ignored him—a skill he was getting better at with each passing day. "We're the group from San Antonio Search and Rescue," he explained. "We were dispatched just this morning."

"Are you that dog's handler?" Julio wanted to know.

"Sí," Luis replied steadily, reaching for his certi-fication. Before he could get the papers Sabrina spoke up.

"Don't judge Dusty by his size . . . he's our best search and rescue dog." Julio blinked, and Luis translated.

"Estoy seguro," Julio said with a responding nod. *I'm sure.* He raised a hand and pointed to a pair of smaller tents about seventy-five yards away. "Find yourselves a cot and get something to eat. Sleep if you can. Someone will be there who can update you." Another man in uniform—dirty and exhausted—stepped up to Julio, and it was clear there was no time for further questions.

The humans and their canines picked their way along the street to the tented area.

"Not the warmest of welcomes," Sabrina mumbled.

"You can't really blame them," Paul replied. "I mean, look what they're dealing with."

The team walked painfully slowly through crowds of people, fallen trees, dust, and heavy equipment. Once they made it to the tents, they split up and stepped around and over makeshift cots and bed pallets on the ground, searching for a few spots they could claim as their own. After what seemed like a long time they found an unclaimed section. There were only two cots and they sagged badly, but there was a pallet on the ground. It was better than nothing, and as good as it was going to get. They were settling in when a woman approached.

"Welcome," she said in halting English. "I'm Marcella. Thank you so much for coming with your dogs." If she noticed Dusty at all, she didn't reveal it. Luis could tell that she was drained. "We're focusing our live searches on six different collapsed buildings within a four-block radius," she said. Everyone understood that "blocks" was being used loosely, because the streets here were not aligned or square like they were in many towns and cities in the United States, and because it was no simple thing to walk from one place to another right now. Getting *anywhere* at all was a challenge.

"Luis and Dusty and Sabrina and Thor will be searching the town's escuela primaria—the primary school. Thirty-six people are still unaccounted for there," she said, reading from a paper on her clipboard. She went on to explain that twenty-eight hours had passed since the earthquake struck. "We're looking for *live* victims," she said soberly. There was still hope, but the clock was ticking.

Luis felt a full-on wave of panic as he listened to Marcella. Primary school. They would be searching the primary school. Both of his nieces—Alejandra and Valentina—were in primary school. But which one? He had no idea.

Dusty nosed Luis's leg, and Luis managed to refocus on Marcella, reminding himself that she had important information he needed to hear.

"Right now the teams working the school have been on the job for over nine hours, and we plan to give them a break sometime after midnight." She paused and looked Luis in the eye. "Are you ready?" Clearly she could sense his trepidation.

Dusty nosed Luis's leg, more firmly this time, and then lifted himself onto his hind legs to balance his front paws on Luis's knee. He could sense his handler's anxiety, too. Luis smelled sour, like worry. But it wasn't time for worry. It was time for work!

Luis thumbed the scar on Dusty's ear and swallowed. He had to put his emotions aside. He had to think logically and be strong. He actually had no idea if his nieces were victims. And even if they were, there were many, many more, each of them a beloved member of *somebody's* family. He looked around at the devastation just outside the tent walls. He had to focus on the big picture, on doing his job. There were people out there who needed their help, and helping was what he'd trained for.

Helping was the reason he and Dusty were here.

28

When Marcella departed, the San Antonio team tried to settle into their little space. Though it was tempting to dive in and get to work, they knew they had a specific job to do, and taking on anything extra would create disorganization and put their mission at risk. It was important to follow protocol and instructions given by the folks in charge.

"So dusty," Sabrina murmured. "And I don't mean the dog!" Indeed, everything was covered in a thick layer of debris dust, which they swept off the cots as best they could. Since Luis and Sabrina would be the first out, they each got a cot, and Laura and Paul shared the pallet on the ground.

Luis checked his phone one last time—nothing—and sent a final text to his brother to tell him where he was. They weren't in his brother's pueblo—he lived about five miles away in a smaller village. He hoped things were not as bad there.

Dusty turned a double circle and curled up next to Luis. He did his best to ignore the dust that was tickling his nose, burying it in the folds of Luis's jacket. It only helped a little. Finally Luis put his phone in his pocket and his arm around Dusty. Dusty snuggled against him, and they both closed their eyes and tried to sleep, though it was basically impossible. The whole group was restless. There was the insidious dust and the smell of destruction. And the sounds! Dusty's ears twitched constantly. Trucks rumbled. People shouted. Sirens wailed. Finally Dusty drifted off, but sleep provided no relief. He dreamed he was back to roaming the streets, alone, looking for food. His stomach twisted with hunger. Darkness hung heavily. Boots kicked cruelly. Headlights glared menacingly. The smell of burning rubber permeated everything.

Lying awake, Luis was glad Dusty was resting but recognized an uneasy sleep. As the minutes and hours ticked by, the din continued relentlessly, punctuated by siren wails. Luis's trepidation grew. He wished that their first mission was simpler . . . less intense. Not so loaded. He also wished they weren't paired with Sabrina and Thor. Though things had settled somewhat between the two, he felt more comfortable with Paul and Laura. Dusty whimpered in his sleep, and Luis stroked his back.

He hoped they were up for this.

Just as Luis finally began to doze, Marcella came to tell them it was time. Luis's watch read three a.m. He was running on twenty-two hours with almost no sleep, a fact he tried to ignore. Doing something was certainly better than doing nothing, even if he had to do it running on fumes. He and Sabrina quickly gathered up their gear and followed Marcella and Laura out of the tent. The sky was dark and heavy with clouds, which reflected the headlights of the vehicles and tall generator-powered lights emergency crews had set up, casting a spooky glow on the already eerie scene. Luis knew a slight chance of rain was in the forecast, and that a light mist would keep the dust down but also make for slippery conditions.

It took half an hour to get to the school site, and the scene was chaotic. Frantic parents were huddled together near a fence line, waiting for news of their children. A traumatized man was screaming at the police. Luis could hear the cop telling the man it wasn't safe for families to search—their job was to keep people safe. They were doing all they could. The best the families could do was stay back and wait. Luis felt for the man and also the cop. The situation was awful for everyone.

The team was introduced to the site leader, Eduardo. "Thank you all for coming," Eduardo said. "We need the backup."

"Happy to be here and ready to assist," Sabrina said. Thor sat at her side, his eyes eager. If he could, he would have said the same thing.

"Right now we're searching on the south side of the building, where several classrooms are, or were, located. They've found three children alive so far. With so many missing we suspect there are more."

Luis struggled to focus as Eduardo spoke. He was dimly aware that nothing was being reported about casualties, though there must have been multiple. The two handlers and their German shepherds from a northern Mexico search and rescue team, the team that they'd be replacing, approached at a snail's pace. To say they looked beleaguered was a drastic understatement. The men were filthy, their foreheads and cheeks stained with sweat beneath their helmets, but that was nothing compared to the fatigue that oozed from their sagging bodies. The dogs panted endlessly, and one of them was limping.

The shepherds towered over Dusty, who appeared smaller than ever next to the mountain of debris that had recently been a school. Dusty's nose quivered at the smell of the dogs as he stood next to their massive shapes. His ears ached already from the wails and shouts and generator motors, and the humming lights that pierced the darkness like headlights in the sky.

For the first time in his life Dusty felt small.

"I've got to get Estrella to the medical tent," the handler with the limping dog said. "I think she's got something stuck between her pads."

"Okay, let's get her over there," Eduardo said, nodding. "And hope it's nothing more serious."

Luis was giving himself a serious internal pep talk when, out of the blue, an aftershock rocked the area. A massive roar filled the air as the search area convulsed, sending debris shifting and sliding for several seconds amid human screams. The lights flickered, plunging everything into momentary darkness. Dusty shivered and barked. Luis held his breath. It lasted only a few seconds, but it felt like an eternity. When it stopped everyone looked around, eyes wide with panic, to see what had changed. Nobody appeared hurt . . . or at least nobody new.

As the cries of the people began to fade Luis heard someone call his name. He turned, recognizing the voice.

"Paco!" he called as his little brother stepped into his arms. They embraced, holding each other tightly for several seconds. As they pulled apart Luis spotted his brother's wife, Marina.

"Your daughters?" Luis choked out. He couldn't make himself form the sentence.

Paco's eyes were wide with shock and horror but shifted to show that he still had gratitude for small mercies. "They're safe," he said, clasping his hands together. "They're with their abuela, Marina's mama. We came so we can help the other children."

His eyes drifted to the mass of concrete and wood and brick and metal lit up by the spotlights. Neither of them said a word for a long moment, silently praying that they would be able to save the poor souls trapped in the twisted prison.

"That's why we're here, too." Luis blinked back salty tears. "Dusty and I are about to get to work."

Paco seemed to notice for the first time that his brother was dressed in rescue gear—that he was part of the rescue team. He looked down at Dusty, his eyes hopeful. He said nothing about his size.

Luis squeezed his brother's arm one last time before turning back to Eduardo and the group.

Eduardo was listening to reports on his walkie-talkie and clearly making adjustments as a result of the aftershock. Luis listened in, suddenly keenly aware of how essential every bit of information was. His worries had disappeared, and he absorbed the communication like a sponge. He knew what he and Dusty were capable of. He couldn't promise that they would find anyone alive, but he could promise that they'd use all of their strength and skill to try.

It was all anyone could do.

29

While the team waited for Eduardo to give final instructions, Luis strapped his helmet, and then his headlamp, onto his head. Dusty wouldn't wear a light, or a vest—it was too dangerous given the tight spaces he'd be going into. But it was required for the humans.

Luis tightened the straps on his own vest and crouched down next to Dusty, who was shivering slightly in the lights. Pulling the booties out of his pocket, he slipped them onto Dusty's feet. When they were secure, he lifted the Chihuahua's chin and looked him in the eye.

"It's time, Dusty," he said. "This is what we've been

training for. And I want you to know that there isn't a doubt about you—or us—in my mind, little dude. Podemos hacerlo," he said. We can do this.

Dusty steadied himself and raised his chin in agreement. "Yip!" he said. Yes! Yes we can!

Luis nodded and strapped on Dusty's doggles. Dusty looked around, adjusting to the lenses.

"Okay, it's time," Eduardo reported. "Everyone ready?"

"Yip!" Dusty replied.

Luis straightened and turned on his headlamp, while Sabrina did the same. The handlers hugged briefly for good luck. They both knew they'd need it.

"Ready," they said in unison.

Sabrina and Thor, with his long, powerful legs, were first to set foot on the collapsed structure. Thor angled right and climbed a solid-looking section of sloping concrete flooring.

Luis and Dusty had been instructed to go left, and aim lower. Luis paused to evaluate the area Eduardo had told them to search, remembering something Roxanne told him weeks ago. Dusty was different, and should search differently. Behaving and searching like a typically sized rescue dog wouldn't highlight his skills, or serve anyone. It could even be dangerous.

Luis's eyes scanned the crumbled building, trying to hone in on areas with smaller spaces between the rebar and concrete, moving slowly and carefully along the edge. Dusty got it right away and moved in front, his nose high. He was zeroing in on something else—smells. And one smell in particular: live human.

He approached the mountain of rubble and leaped lightly onto a teetering beam that spanned a crevasse, gingerly making his way across. Once he was safely on the other side, he hopped over a pipe and walked along a chunk of rebar-enforced flooring. Luis followed as closely as he could, but was soon halted. At 195 pounds he weighed more than twenty times his partner's weight, and his heaviness caused the unsteady terrain beneath him to shift almost immediately. Dusty stopped and turned back, clearly looking for permission. He knew it was his job to forge ahead but couldn't do it without the okay. He locked eyes with Luis, and Luis nodded at him. And then came the words Dusty needed, and loved, to hear: "Go search!"

Dusty kept moving, sniffing his way over and around massive piles of splintered wood, rebar, pipes, and concrete, while Luis stuck to a lower edge and kept his partner in sight as best he could. Every once in a while Luis spotted a piece of broken furniture from a classroom—a desk top, a broken chair, and even a giant, unbroken chalkboard. It was too much to think about . . . classrooms full of children just forty-eight hours ago, now reduced to this.

Finally Luis found another, sturdier way up the rubble pile and climbed, grateful for every moment of agility practice he'd put in on the Sterling ranch. Once he was a little higher he could see Dusty, about twenty yards away, sniffing intently at a tiny crack in a broken wall.

The wall, Luis noticed immediately, was tilted at a crazy angle. He could never get up there safely, and neither could a full-sized dog. But Dusty weighed almost nothing, so he could. Luis could see Dusty's nose quivering. He hoped he smelled something!

Dusty's nose had taken on a life of its own. The bothersome dust was barely a thing anymore . . . he smelled something else! The opening here was small—even for him—but he knew for certain that there were people down there. Maybe even live people.

He raised his head, his ears twitching, his eyes finding Luis. Dawn was approaching, but it was still dim. Even under the emergency lights he couldn't see his partner clearly . . . mostly his shadow and his body language. It was enough. Dusty could tell that Luis was urging him on just from his posture. His giant ears rotated slightly, waiting for the words.

"Good boy, Dusty," Luis called. "Go search!"

Dusty felt energy surge up his spine. He gazed into the narrow tunnel, blinking behind his doggles. His nose quivered. Stepping forward, he squeezed his body inside.

30

The weak predawn light disappeared as Dusty made his way into the wreckage, leaving him in almost total darkness. The passage was narrow, too narrow for a person or any other dog. The tiny Chihuahua had only a few inches of clearance on either side as he inched forward. He placed each paw carefully, testing to make sure the ground beneath him was solid. The way the ground had recently trembled and grumbled and growled like an angry beast had been frightening. Some things weren't supposed to move—like the earth under your paws. He'd never felt anything like it before, and hoped he never would again.

Pausing, Dusty inhaled and confirmed that he could still smell what had caught his attention on the surface. It was a slightly stale scent but unmistakable and one of his favorites. He smelled children. He tried to ignore the other scents that entered his sensitive snout along with the smell of people . . . smells like blood and fear.

The darkness made him uncomfortable. The feeling sat along his spine like a coiled spring, making him anxious to move faster. Only months and months of training to slow down—and reassurances from Roxanne and Luis—kept the feeling from making him rush forward. Instead he continued slowly and carefully down a long, straight path just wide enough for him to balance on. It was a long piece of debris from the collapse, perhaps a beam that had crashed down. He moved with intention, the way he had been trained. It took every ounce of self-control in his little Chihuahua frame. Holding still, he sniffed again. He did not want to waste a single step in this strange cave of devastation. He was here to *find*, to find and to get out.

After a few more steps, Dusty's ears brushed the top of the narrowing passage. He shrunk down and willed himself to be even smaller. Without enough space to turn around, all he could do was go forward. The rough edges of broken concrete and sharp steel scraped at his sides. Still he wriggled onward, stretching out his paws and pulling himself along. The only consolation in the close dark was the smell still drifting up the constricting path—it was getting stronger!

Dusty resisted the urge to bark. He hadn't reached his target. He extended his paws and felt something blocking the way ahead. He pushed with his back feet, trying to propel himself forward. His toes caught in thin wires snaking out of the broken walls. He yanked his foot, but the tangled wires tightened and dug in. He stifled a yelp. He wanted out of this claustrophobic space! He wanted to be on the pillow beside Luis, or in Shelby's lap, or curled up with his siblings beside his warm mama!

Dusty stopped. He breathed in. He smelled the scent of children again, stronger now, and let it soothe him. He also smelled something else . . . a faint whisper of fresher air.

Then very carefully, almost without moving, Dusty wriggled his back paw until it came loose. He was free. He could keep going, and he would. The black tip of Dusty's nose quivered. He was close. So close.

Moving to one side, just slightly, Dusty was able to get himself to a spot where the passage widened slightly and he could walk again. The beam he'd been following ended abruptly, and the space grew larger still, though it was just as dark. He fought the urge to race forward. Carefully, carefully, he continued.

His eyes were wide in the darkness, desperate for a hint of light. At last he saw a glimmer. Tiny shafts of weak sunlight were finding their way to him. He stepped around a corner, and the smell of kids and fresher air grew stronger. There! In the dim gloom he could make out the shapes of three humans—three children—slumped against a steeply leaning column and surrounded by concrete and pieces of broken furniture.

Dusty scampered over to them, unable to move

slowly now that he could see his target! The ceiling was too low for the children to stand, but Dusty could move freely. He approached each child cautiously, listening for breath. He could smell that they were alive, but they weren't moving. He nosed each body in turn but got no response. The children needed help. That's what he was here for. So he sat down beside the closest child and did exactly what he was trained to do—he barked. He barked and barked and barked.

31

Perched on the edge of the destruction heap, Luis worried. He paced back and forth on a small piece of solid plywood. It took all of his will not to leap into the pile that had recently been a school and start digging in the spot where Dusty's little flag of a tail had disappeared into the debris. It had been a long time since he'd gone in. Too long.

Luis sank onto his haunches, touching one hand to the dirt. He listened as hard as he could. He waited to hear a bark, a whimper, a footstep . . . anything. The search site was noisy, and getting noisier as the sun rose and more and more teams came to help. Firefighters, police, military personnel, construction workers with large machines, and even concerned citizens flooded the search sites. They came from all walks of life and wore the same frustrated and haunted expressions, especially in their eyes. They wanted to do *something* to make the situation better, to help, to save victims. Many understood that with each second that ticked by, the chances of finding people alive grew slimmer.

Luis let the sounds of the rescue workers console him. He reminded himself that everyone was doing what they could, including Dusty. He closed his eyes and rubbed his temples. The din of people and machines suddenly went silent. Opening his eyes, Luis looked up and saw a man in yellow safety gear on the pile. He was holding his fist high in a call for silence. Someone, somewhere had heard something! He put his own fist in the air—the sign that told everyone to stop whatever they were doing to listen.

Luis's ears rang with the silence. He strained to hear . . . something. Seconds passed. Thirty. Sixty. Everyone waited, on edge and ready to focus their efforts on an area where they might find somebody alive. Finally the man in yellow put his arm down. The rest of the arms soon dropped as well. It was a false alarm. Whatever they thought they heard, they had not heard again. The general search resumed.

Cautiously Luis climbed the pile to the crack Dusty had entered. He leaned as close as he could and wished for the thousandth time that human ears weren't so useless. He wondered, if he called out, would Dusty hear him? He wanted to let Dusty know he had his back. That he was right here, waiting. He knew it would be a mistake to call the dog's name. Dusty needed to be wherever he was, doing his job. Sometimes the hardest part of SAR work was letting a partner do his job.

Luis was reaching for his water bottle when he froze. There. He thought he heard the sound he'd been waiting for—a familiar bark. He waited, wanting to hear it again and afraid that his mind was playing tricks. He looked around at the people nearby to see if they had heard it, too.

A Mexican navy rescuer stilled among the chunks of concrete he'd been lifting. "Did you hear something?" he asked, catching Luis's concerned look. Luis squinted up at the man. The sun was higher and the worker was standing in the light. Luis nodded. Yes, he did.

The worker, standing higher on the pile, shouted and held his fist in the air. "¡Puños arriba!" All around them, people repeated the movement. They stopped moving. Stopped talking. Stopped looking. Engines were shut off, and everyone listened with fists raised. It was almost silent.

Luis felt his heart stop before it began pounding again, furiously and in time with the barks of the bravest dog he knew.

"Yip! Yip! Yip! Yip!" It was Dusty. He was alerting him. He was alerting them all. He had found people alive!

32

Dusty sneezed and kept barking. His snout and throat were filled with dust, but he wouldn't let that stop him. He *couldn't* let that stop him. "Yip, yip, yip, YIP!"

The three children he'd found were still immobile, but one of them was conscious. She'd woken up when Dusty began barking. He sat as close to her as he could so she could feel the heat of his body and know he was there. He understood she wasn't fully aware of him but that staying close was good. His spirits lifted when she raised her hand and weakly touched his back.

Between barks, Dusty nosed the hands of the other

two, hoping they would wake up as well. One of them moaned softly.

Pausing in his alert, Dusty listened to the noises coming from above. They had stopped briefly but were now growing louder. He could hear scraping concrete. Shouts. Motors. And Luis! He barked and barked and barked. The timbre of his partner's voice was as unmistakable as his smell . . . Luis was coming for him! For all of them.

After several attempts to locate the spot closest to the sound of Dusty's barking, the rescue crew had zeroed in. Because victims could only survive inside small pockets within a collapsed structure, it was too dangerous to use big diggers to move the debris quickly. The risk of an excavator could trigger another collapse. Instead the building fragments had to be removed painstakingly slowly, by hand. But now that they had a target, the effort could remain focused. Luis worked with the rest of the available workers forming human chains, passing bricks, wood, buckets of rubble, and chunks of pipe and concrete from person to person, moving pieces of the destroyed school off the pile. A few people with hand tools carefully broke up big pieces. A single backhoe working with a spotter was used to lift the largest pieces from the pile. Each enormous chunk was strung up on wires and carefully lifted and swung away. With each load they inched closer to their goal. The barking grew louder.

Luis swallowed his impatience and continued to pry, lift, and haul away every scrap he could. He was still anxious, but at least now he was occupied, and helping!

In the dark hollow, Dusty barked less and less . . . just enough to let the rescuers know they were on the right path. He could hear them getting closer!

Suddenly Dusty's hair stood on end. He heard the deep distant growl before anyone else. It sounded exactly like the one he'd heard before! A few seconds later a strong aftershock hit, making the ground pitch and buckle. Dust and small chunks of debris rained down on Dusty and the victims. The girl cried out in terror. Dusty trembled, unable to bark.

All at once it was over. The aftershock stopped as

quickly as it had started. The earth quieted. Atop the massive heap, the rescue crews were also quiet as dust rose off the pile. Everyone stood frozen, waiting. Then they heard it: the brave bark of the Chihuahua.

Luis let his breath out in a gush. Dusty had not been crushed by the shifting pile. He was still in there. Alive! And doing his job. But they needed to get to him and the victims before the unsettled earth shook again.

Grabbing a chunk of concrete, Luis used all his strength to hoist it up. A woman in a hardhat and safety vest caught the other end before it toppled, and together they moved it off the pile. They were one layer closer to Dusty and the victims.

33

Time passed more quickly now that Luis was actively working, but still seemed to trickle by.

"Here." A woman in a green vest who'd been working nearby for the last few hours handed him a bottle. Luis paused, mopped his brow, and accepted the water. He'd been working for six hours. Sabrina and Thor had been called off, replaced by the next team. When Laura had radioed to tell Luis he should take a break, he'd refused. "I'm staying until we reach Dusty," he told her. "I won't quit while he's still working."

The Incident Command leader hesitated. It was her job to make sure that the dogs and handlers were cared for. If they got too hungry, tired, or stressed, they could make an already dangerous situation worse. She knew where Luis was coming from, though. She was a handler, too. And handlers stick with their dog. "Be safe," she told Luis, and signed off.

Luis took a second swallow of water, which did nothing to clear the sandy feeling in his throat that came with zero sleep and an excess of dust and smoke. The day was warm and would soon be hot. Capping the bottle, he heard a cry from the rescuers and saw several men waving their arms, motioning him closer. There'd been a breakthrough!

Within minutes someone arrived with a long ladder that they lowered slowly into a murky opening. People on the edges arranged the rubble in attempts to shore up the unstable pile. Then, slowly, the way he had watched his dog do it, Luis placed his feet carefully and moved down the ladder. He was only a few steps in, followed by an emergency medical technician, when Dusty barked again so loudly it made Luis grin.

"Dusty!" At last he could call his dog's name.

Luis's eyes adjusted and Dusty jumped and spun in small circles near his feet. "Good dog, Dusty," Luis told him. He reached down and gave him a quick pat. He'd have liked to snatch him up, climb out of the volatile cavern, and do nothing but play tug and administer belly rubs for the rest of the day, but their job wasn't done . . . not yet. He crouched down and moved with the tech and firefighter to the three living victims. There was no time to waste.

The EMT assessed the children as quickly as she could, mobilizing to get them out. All of them were exhausted and dehydrated and traumatized. Since there was no way of knowing the extent of their injuries, all three were secured to backboards and carried up and out. The conscious girl was disoriented and had a large bump on her head—possibly a concussion. It was good that Dusty had helped keep her awake. The black-haired boy sitting in the middle had a broken leg that needed stabilizing before he could be moved. The third child, breathing but limp, had lost a lot of blood from a puncture in her thigh and was rushed away for a transfusion.

Dusty spent only a moment with Luis. He was elated to see him and also aware that they were still working. He ran back to the two remaining children as they were loaded onto stretchers, offering small licks. He would not leave them alone until they were out, safe and getting the care they needed.

Dusty and Luis stood in the gloomy wreckage until everyone else was out. "Okay," Luis said.

This time Dusty did not slow himself down at all. He bounded up the ladder, his paws barely touching the rails, and raced into the sunshine with a victory bark. He jumped around the opening, licking Luis's face as he emerged.

Luis had never been happier to kiss a dog. His radio crackled, and the duo heard Laura's familiar voice. She'd been marking the progress and getting reports, and knew the team was out. It was time for them to get checked out by their own medical attendants. Time to get some rest. "I'm not taking no for an answer this time," she told Luis.

Luis lifted Dusty and pulled Bear from a vest pocket, offering it to him. He felt the small dog who loved to walk on his own feet relax in his arms. They were both exhausted. "We did it," Luis whispered. "Good dog." Of course he knew the job wasn't finished—there was still a lot of work to do. But they had found three living people, and that was incredible.

He started the slow walk back to the base. All around them people stopped their work. They clapped their hands together for the tiny hero dog and his big man partner. They patted Luis on the back. They reached out to pet Dusty. Several were crying.

"Gracias," they heard again and again. Finding three children alive had given everyone the hope they needed to keep going.

"¡Hermano!" Paco rushed up to his brother and embraced him. "You are a hero!"

"Dusty is the hero," Luis said.

"Dusty." Paco shook his head, amazed by the little perrito. "You are tesoro."

34

"Hold on a sec, okay? I've got another call coming in," Shelby told Ryan before putting him on hold. She looked at the number blinking on the screen and realized that it was an international call, from Mexico. They hadn't received one of those since . . .

"Oh my gosh!" Shelby whispered to herself. "Hello?" she said, half holding her breath. The phone crackled with bad reception.

"Is this the Sterling ranch?" a deep voice asked through the buzzing.

"Luis, is that you?" Shelby half shouted.

Luis let out a chuckle. "Sí, it's me. I wanted to call and tell you about Dusty's first mission."

"Hold on!" Shelby cried a second time. She switched back to Ryan and explained that she had to go. "I'll call you back! It's Dusty on the other line!"

Ryan laughed aloud. "Now the miracle Chihuahua can talk?" he quipped.

"Oh, no!" Shelby babbled. "It's really Luis. I just meant—"

"I see how it is," Ryan continued to tease. "I'm only your number one until a certain Chihuahua calls you up!"

Shelby was smiling, getting it, and glad Ryan's feelings weren't hurt. "I'll call you back!" she promised before clicking off and hitting the intercom button that connected the welcome center to the canine pavilion. "Luis and Dusty are on the line! Come quick!"

Unable to wait, Shelby begged Luis to fill her in.

"He was incredible," Luis reported. "He crawled into a tiny crack and was out of sight for several hours. He found three unconscious children, and all three are going to be fine. Everyone is calling it a miracle!"

As Shelby listened she could almost feel the warmth of Dusty sitting in her lap. Of him licking her hand, or strutting across the floor. That tiny, mangy little puppy had transformed himself—with help, of course—into a hero.

Blinking, Shelby realized that she was crying tears of happiness. She wiped her cheeks with the back of her hand, sniffling. By the time her family and Pablo made it to the welcome center she had dark streaks running all the way down her cheeks.

"Oh no," Pablo said, alarmed.

"It is bad news?" Forrest asked.

Shelby shook her head. "He's a hero!" she shouted, and put Luis on speaker so he could tell the tale again.

"Yip!" Dusty barked in the background.

While faces exploded into expressions of happiness and excitement, Morgan watched her older sister a bit warily. When Luis finished telling the story a second time, she walked over and whispered, "Shelby, your mascara is running. Um . . . badly." Shelby blinked back her happy tears, her face exploding into the widest grin Morgan had ever seen on her sister's face.

"Who cares?" Shelby cried. "Dusty is a rescue dog of giants!"

Pedro handed Shelby a tissue, nodding. "Thank goodness Sylvia didn't mistake that little pooch for a piece of dusty roadside trash," he said. "That little perro is pure treasure."

A NOTE FROM THE AUTHORS

As bona fide dog lovers we jumped at the opportunity to write stories about rescue dogs. Knowing that the project would require extensive research, we excitedly explored websites, books, articles, and anything else that could help us learn about rescue dog training, handler pairing, and the disasters dogs assist with. We found dozens of inspiring stories about real dogs doing what they do best: acting selflessly, loyally, enthusiastically, tirelessly, and heroically to save people in peril. We were won over by these incredible tales of canines and their companions, and inspired by the dedication and hard work so many two- and four-legged creatures undertake in service of others. We also learned that there are many differing theories and methods of dog training.

It can take years of training and discipline to develop dogs' natural gifts into skills that make them both safe and effective helpers in the aftermath of disasters. Dozens of canine search and rescue agencies all over the world do this important work, and while they all share the common goal of creating well-matched and successful dog and handler teams, each has its own philosophy and style. There is no single path to becoming a certified search dog. Though we were particularly inspired by the National Disaster Search Dog Foundation, established by Wilma Melville and her Labrador, Murphy, we pulled from several schools of thought regarding both training and searching to create these dog-inspired fictional stories. We hope you enjoy them. Woof!

ABOUT THE AUTHORS

Jane B. Mason and Sarah Hines Stephens are co-authors of several middle-grade novels, including the A Dog and His Girl Mysteries series and the Candy Apple titles *The Sister Switch* and *Snowfall Surprise*. As Sarah Jane they wrote the critically acclaimed *Maiden Voyage: A Titanic Story*. *Ember* was the first book in their Rescue Dogs series.

DON'T MISS THE FIRST BOOK IN THE RESCUE DOGS SERIES!